"While we were waiting for our order, I saw a man. He was watching us."

Cade's gut feeling had solidified. Over her shoulder, he studied the diner's facade. Tori turned to see what he was looking at. What scant color there was left in her face drained, and she lifted a trembling hand to clutch her neck.

"Cade..."

Only one of the plate-glass windows had been blown out. Theirs.

"My car. It wasn't an accident, was it?" Her gaze swerved to his, begging him to refute her claim.

"We can't know that for sure—"

"Someone *shot* at us. This isn't Chicago or New York City. This is small-town America." She had to work to drag in air. "You told me not to ignore my instincts. I should've heeded your advice. Someone has been watching me since I returned. Waiting for an opportunity to—"

She didn't finish the sentence. Didn't have to.

They both knew that, had the timing been different yesterday, had the shooter's aim been a little more accurate, Tori would be dead already.

Karen Kirst was born and raised in east Tennessee near the Great Smoky Mountains. She's a lifelong lover of books, but it wasn't until after college that she had the grand idea to write one herself. Now she divides her time between being a wife, homeschooling mom and romance writer. Her favorite pastimes are reading, visiting tearooms and watching romantic comedies.

Visit the Author Profile page at Harlequin.com for more titles.

EXPLOSIVE REUNION

KAREN KIRST

HARLEQUIN® LOVE INSPIRED® SUSPENSE

Recycling programs for this product may not exist in your area.

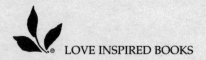 LOVE INSPIRED BOOKS

ISBN-13: 978-1-335-23187-1

Explosive Reunion

www.Harlequin.com

Printed in U.S.A.

Fear thou not; for I am with thee: be not dismayed;
for I am thy God: I will strengthen thee;
yea, I will help thee; yea, I will uphold thee
with the right hand of my righteousness.
–Isaiah 41:10

To the men and women of our armed forces
who serve our country, and to their families
who love and support them. Thank you for your service,
dedication and sacrifice.

A huge thank-you to my own marine, Marek.
I'm proud to be your wife.

Thank you to my editor, Emily Rodmell,
and to Love Inspired executive editor Tina James for
giving me the opportunity to switch gears from historical
romance to romantic suspense. It's been a blast!

Thank you to my Lord and Savior, Jesus Christ,
who walked with me during the writing of this book
and gave me the confidence and ability to complete it.

Acknowledgments

Thank you to Sergeant Dan Morton for patiently answering
my law enforcement questions. And thanks to
Jessica Felker, RN, BSN, my niece and a wonderful nurse,
for assisting me with medical information.
Any mistakes are purely my own.

ONE

Sneads Ferry, North Carolina

Marines didn't tuck tail and run at the first hint of trouble. They didn't panic. They assessed problems and devised practical solutions. Ten years of service had honed Staff Sergeant Cade McMann's skills and cemented his confidence. He should be able to have a simple conversation with his ex-fiancée without trembling in his boots.

When he'd learned Tori James was moving back to their small fishing community, he'd known there'd be adjustments. But she'd been home a month, and pretending they didn't share a painful history—and attempting to avoid each other despite their families' close ties—had become a problem. Time to deal with it.

As he approached her place, a gray-and-white Queen Anne home set in a narrow lot, house flags whipped in the wind and chimes clattered a discordant alarm. The sign advertising Tori's pet-supply shop swayed on creaking chains. The Canine Companion occupied the first floor. The second had been converted into an apartment years ago. A tinkling bell heralded the exit of a customer and her four-legged pet. She was chatting and laughing with a petite blonde woman.

Tori. His gut tightened.

A humid breeze teased the hem of her flirty summer dress, drawing his eyes to her shapely legs and round-toed flats.

The pair continued across the generous covered porch and into the stamp-sized flower garden surrounded by a low brick wall, the dog trotting between them. She hadn't noticed him yet. Contentment curved her lips as she bent to give the pooch a proper goodbye.

The back of his neck grew hot. The last time he'd been face-to-face with her, she'd ripped his heart from his chest and stomped on it.

It's now or never. "Hello, Tori."

Tori popped up, a strangled cry of surprise catching in her throat. "Cade." Taking in his camouflage uniform and heavy lace-up boots, her brows slammed together. "What are you doing here?"

The other woman's gaze bouncing between them, she guided her dog toward the exit. Cade moved to unlatch the gate and hold it open for her. Once she was out of earshot, he stepped through and let it shuffle closed behind him.

His keys bit into his palm. "Would you believe I'm here to purchase one of those fancy dog cookies?"

"You don't own a dog." Her white-blond hair danced about her face. She'd lopped off several inches, and the pale, straight layers kissed the underside of her jaw. The short style enhanced her delicate bone structure and made her green eyes pop. "Unless you got one and didn't tell your mother."

Best friends for decades, their mothers had few secrets. "I'm pet free at the moment."

"Then I can't help you."

"Let me buy you a cup of coffee."

"It's ninety degrees."

"An ice cream, then. Last I heard, Red's Diner still sells vanilla-and-orange swirl."

At the mention of the diner they'd frequented, the corners of her mouth turned down. "Maybe another time."

When she pivoted and started to walk away, he caught her wrist in a light hold. "Your mom's birthday party is Sunday night." His mom, Dee, had been planning the event for weeks. She wanted to give Barbara a sixtieth birthday celebration that would hopefully get her mind off of her illness. "Do you really believe our families won't be evaluating our every move?"

"I'm sure we can manage to be civil."

"Can we? You aren't even willing to let me buy you an ice cream."

He hadn't been this close to her since she ended their engagement a decade ago. Her perfume, a pleasant blend of oranges and bergamot, transported him to another time, to when they'd been each other's closest confidantes. Friends since middle school, it wasn't until their senior year that he'd realized friendship wasn't enough anymore.

A garbage receptacle toppled over. Tori cringed, her gaze darting around to the neighboring homes.

"Something wrong?"

"I've had a weird feeling these past few days…" She grimaced. "It's nothing. That's what I get for reading back-to-back murder mysteries."

He did his own scan of their surroundings and found nothing out of the ordinary. No one stirred outside the mint-green house next door advertising tax services. Directly across the street, three gardeners worked to tidy the double lot belonging to a swanky bed-and-breakfast.

"Don't dismiss your instincts. If you think—"

"Forget it." She leveled him a look that reminded him that their days of sharing confidences were long gone. "Look, Cade, if you want to talk, let's talk about my brother. You have to convince him not to enlist."

Over the years, Jason had become the little brother Cade never had. When the eighteen-year-old had confided in him about his dreams of a military career, he'd warned him Tori wouldn't be pleased.

"He'll be an asset to the Corps. He's strong, physically and mentally. There are opportunities for advancement, and he can take college courses later on. Your mom gave him her blessing."

He didn't have to ask why she wouldn't. Her experience as a military kid had been characterized by frustration and disappointment. A respected member of Force Recon, her father Thomas James had been involved in secretive missions more often than he was home. His frequent, unexpected absences had put a strain on his marriage and caused his daughter to become disillusioned. After his untimely death—which, to this day, was shrouded in mystery—she used to say that she lost her father to the military long before.

Her eyes flashed. "I know you're married to the Marines, but that doesn't have to be Jason's future."

Cade wrestled with fresh hurt and disappointment that carried him back to the day she'd cut him out of his life. He'd known she wouldn't like his decision to enlist, but he hadn't dreamed she'd refuse to marry him because of it. Their breakup was the reason he'd almost flunked out of boot camp.

The June heat ratcheted up a notch. He tugged off his cover and ran his hand over his hair. "My life may not be perfect, but it's a good one. I'm proud of what I've accomplished. Whether or not Jason joins, it's ultimately his decision, not yours."

"Thank you for reminding me how little you value my opinion," she retorted, hurt glistening in her eyes. "It didn't matter ten years ago. I see nothing's changed."

Tori backed away. He was reviewing the ways he'd messed up when an explosion rocked the ground beneath him. The sound of a nearby lawnmower was eclipsed by the roar of twisting metal. A wave of intense heat billowed toward them. With Tori's scream ringing in his ears, he lunged for her.

Cade's big body pressed Tori into the sunbaked earth, his arm heavy across her back and his cheek tucked against her neck, as bits of fiery debris rained down on them. Brittle grass poked her skin. Her right wrist throbbed.

"What happened?" She tried to move, but her human shield wasn't budging.

"I don't know."

His weight shifted above her, and his exclamation spurred her to take advantage of his distraction. She inched out from underneath him and clapped her hand over her mouth.

Orange flames devoured her car seats. Her rearview mirror dangled in front of what used to be the windshield. Black smoke rolled and curled high into the sky, aiming for the branches high above their heads. Her car was nothing more than a hulled-out shell.

"My car," she breathed, choking on the acrid taste invading her mouth.

Cade curved his arm around her waist and helped her stand. "Are you hurt?"

"I don't understand. How? Why?"

"Tori?" He shoved his face close, his ocean-blue eyes churning.

"I'm fine."

Her car wasn't, though. Rushing out the front gate, she strode to the end of the driveway for a better view.

Cade followed on her heels. She pointed to the detached garage, thankful it was too full of overstock and gardening tools to be used for parking. "Do you see any damage?"

"Nothing obvious." He nodded grimly to the side of the house. "Your upstairs window's broken."

"My bedroom. I should make sure whatever busted the glass doesn't catch the house on fire."

"I'll come with you."

In normal circumstances, she would've refused the offer. Memories of Cade permeated the house. Her mom had purchased it fifteen years ago, when Tori was just thirteen, and transformed the first floor into a paradise for dogs and the second into a rentable apartment. Cade and his family had helped with everything from tagging merchandise to installing bathroom tile. After a renter had been found and the shop opened for business, he'd continued to pitch in whenever he could. He and Tori had swept floors, passed out sales flyers and even convinced Barbara to carry bakery-grade dog cookies.

But right now, Tori appreciated the company. Her heartbeat hadn't yet resumed its usual rhythm and her legs felt rubbery. She kept expecting something else to go boom.

Inside, she ascended the stairs hugging the left of the foyer. Cade's heavier tread pelted behind her. She quickly unlocked the door at the top of the steps and entered the short hallway.

"Doesn't smell like anything is burning." She tapped

a pile of cardboard boxes. "Watch your step. I haven't gotten around to unpacking everything yet."

"You're to be commended, Tori. Leaving your position at the library and your home in Tennessee in order to come back and give your mom a break couldn't have been easy."

The admiration in his eyes put a lump in her throat. "She needed me."

"Not everyone would be willing to make that sacrifice."

While it was true her mom's lupus diagnosis had been the primary motivating factor, there were other reasons she'd craved a break from her life there. Reasons she'd rather keep private.

Tori led the way into the corner room that she'd designated as the master bedroom. Bits of glass littered her bed. A twisted piece of metal lay on her throw rug.

"There's the culprit," she said.

Cade crossed to the broken window and pulled out his phone to call emergency dispatch.

She hung back, soaking in the changes time had wrought. He'd been handsome as a teen, the combination of inky-black hair, vivid blue eyes and a winsome smile earning him scores of admirers. More athletic than studious, he'd possessed an energy that couldn't be tamed. But he hadn't let his popularity go to his head. He'd been kind to everyone, no matter their status, a hero even before he'd donned the uniform. No wonder she'd fallen for him.

He'd matured into an intriguing, gorgeous man. His military regulation haircut, buzzed short on the sides but long enough to run his fingers through on the top, lent him an intimidating edge. He was taller than she remembered. Broader. In top physical condition—able to scale walls, leap out of helicopters, wrestle bad guys or whatever the Marine Corps asked him to do. She really didn't want to know specifics. She'd worried about him during every deployment, praying for his safety and experiencing a rush of relief with every homecoming. Tori may have turned her back on military life, but thanks to her mom's regular reports of Cade's movements, she hadn't escaped the emotional rollercoaster. If Jason enlisted, she'd be worrying about him, too.

He ended the call. "The fire department will be here soon."

She joined him at the window. From this angle, the burning vehicle looked even more ominous. "This isn't commonplace, is it?"

"Commonplace? No. But not impossible, especially considering the age of your vehicle. I doubt it had an electric fan. The catalytic converter could've been clogged. Or there could've been a fuel leak."

Those options sounded reasonable. Far more reasonable than the paths her mind were taking. She had to reconsider her choice of reading material. There was no one after her. She sold pet supplies, not classified information.

Cade turned toward her, his gaze narrowing. "Do you suspect this wasn't an accident?"

"Of course not." That would be ridiculous.

His gaze dropped deliberately to where she was fiddling with her ring. "Is someone giving you trouble? A customer? Neighbor? Boyfriend?"

She studied his face for clues. Did he know about her former boyfriend and the activities that landed him in prison? Tori had made her mom promise not to tell anyone in the McMann family.

"None of the above."

Seemingly satisfied with her answer, he peered through both windows. "People are congregating on the sidewalk."

"I should go down there and reassure my neighbors."

Outside, they found a gathering crowd, shock reflected on their faces. Her next-door neighbor wove his way to her side. "Tori, are you okay?"

Her wrist throbbed and she was without transportation. It wasn't the best day, but it could've been much worse. She was grateful that the house and her mom's beloved shop were still intact.

"I'm fine, Kenneth." She introduced the harried tax man to Cade. The two nodded to each other in greeting. Slightly older than her, the reed-thin bachelor with owlish features seemed to always be at loose ends. But he had a steady stream of customers, so he must be good at his job.

"I was putting my frozen dinner into the microwave when I heard the explosion." Blinking behind the thick glasses, he tried to smooth his riotous curls. "You're fortunate this didn't happen fifteen minutes later."

Cade shifted his stance. "Why do you say that?"

"Tori drives to the bank every day after she closes the store, like clockwork."

He blanched. Their gazes locked, and the questions surging in his eyes mirrored her own. Who else besides Kenneth had taken note of her habits? Had the destruction of her car been, in fact, an act of deliberate violence?

TWO

"Don't say it, Cade." Tori wrapped her arms around her midsection.

"You have to admit the timing is suspicious," he murmured.

"It's a coincidence."

She was a regular citizen. A librarian. Except she'd temporarily traded books for pet supplies.

Before he could respond, the whine of sirens careened around the corner. A fire engine rumbled to a stop in the middle of the street, followed by several patrol cars. Cade remained by her side as firefighters doused the flames. By the looks of the darkening sky, rain would've soon taken care of it.

Deputy Wayne Claxton introduced himself and wrote her information on a palm-sized paper pad. About the age her father would be if he'd lived, the wire-haired, mustached deputy had perfected his poker face, not giving so much as a hint of his thoughts.

"Your car wasn't running, correct?"

"That's right."

"Did you see or smell evidence of a fire before the explosion?"

She'd been too distracted by Cade to notice. "No."

"You haven't had any electrical issues? Problems with your ignition switch?"

"No, nothing like that. I take it in for routine maintenance."

He put away his pad and promised to contact her with the fire department's investigation results, which he warned would take several days. The tow truck was departing when she felt the first raindrops on her exposed skin.

Cade squinted toward the sky. "You have anything to cover that window?"

Tori's hesitation vanished at the peal of thunder. "Maybe in the garage."

In the month since she'd returned, she'd split her time between unpacking and manning the shop, so she hadn't had time to check out the garage. They quickly rifled through the contents and discovered a couple of sheets of plywood against the rear wall. He also located an electric drill.

In her bedroom once again, they worked together to clear the glass and debris. Wind whistled through the gap. Rain splattered the sill.

While Tori supported the plywood, he drilled the screws along the edges. "Feels like old times. Us doing chores," he said, his attention on his task. "You gonna pay me in Popsicles like your mom used to do?"

"Sorry. I'm fresh out."

He grunted and continued working.

She studied his profile, the proud line of his forehead and the jut of his cheekbones. His features had been branded on her mind years ago. Granted, he was even more handsome now than he'd been at eighteen.

He'd once been her closest confidante. When her feelings for him had shifted to something more, she'd kept them hidden for fear of losing his friendship. Remaining silent while he dated other girls was one of the hardest things she'd had to do. Then, on the night of their senior prom, Cade's kiss had changed everything. That summer, they'd whiled away the days playing in the surf, crabbing in the river and counting stars from her front-porch swing. She'd begun to think of the future in terms of her and Cade as a couple. Instead of heading to a prestigious university as her mother expected, she enrolled in the community college. Cade was supposed to follow in his father's footsteps and assume the family fishing business. He hadn't questioned his path, so neither had she.

His proposal had come earlier than expected, but that hadn't stopped her from saying yes. Cade was her soul mate. Her best friend. Her heart was safe with him.

Or so she'd believed, until the day he'd found her in the college library and delivered the earth-shattering news that he'd enlisted. Signed a four-year contract to serve their country and be at the Marine Corps' beck and call.

With that day fresh in her mind, her heart throbbed with remembered betrayal.

She wouldn't be that vulnerable again.

Cade lowered the drill and inspected his work. "Should hold until we can get you a new window."

"I appreciate your help."

"Is there someone who can take you to the hardware store?"

Jason worked night shifts at a local factory, and she didn't want to burden her mom. Barbara needed to rest and focus on managing her illness. Tori's close friend, Angela Reagan, was probably pulling a twelve-hour shift at the hospital.

"I could contact someone from my church."

"Or you could let me give you a ride," he said casually. "My Jeep's parked at the bank down the street."

More time in Cade's company. Great. "Let me get the deposit ready." She sighed.

Cade began cleaning up the glass. As Tori descended the stairs, a sharp clap of thunder reverberated through the house. The lights flickered out. Startled, her foot slipped, and she grabbed the railing to keep from tumbling down the steep flight.

She reached the bottom tread and sucked in a steadying breath. Shadows draped the foyer and hallway leading to the rear of the house. Weak light slanted into the parlor across from her, the first room customers encountered and the largest on this floor. Tori skirted the large round table in the middle boasting individual dog treats of every shape and color to get to the counter and her register.

A sudden gust of rain pelted the window behind her. She clapped a hand over her mouth.

She was being silly. There was no reason to be on edge.

The leather pouch she used to transport her daily earnings wasn't in its usual spot. Tori must've left it in the office that morning. She walked through the archway connecting the parlor to what used to be the formal dining room. Flashes of lightning illuminated the shelves and collections of leashes and collars. It wasn't yet seven o'clock, but gloom had descended along with the storm. Hopefully the power outage wouldn't last too long. Already, the air was growing heavy with humidity.

She entered the former-kitchen-turned-office and immediately the hairs on her nape stood to attention. She reached for the light switch before catching herself. No electricity.

Outside, the storm unleashed its fury. The oaks'

branches thrashed the sides of the house. A crash sent adrenaline spiraling through her system. Calling herself a fool, she marched to the door and, ripping it open, emerged onto the screened porch. Wind tunneled through the screens, twisting her dress hem about her knees. Rain gushed through the gutters and onto the pavers.

A faint scuffling sound registered near the left side of the house. Tori pivoted that direction and caught sight of a hunched figure dashing behind her garage.

Cade carried the box of discarded glass downstairs. The silence inside the house was at complete odds with the fury beyond the walls. Good thing they'd gotten the plywood in place in time.

"Tori?"

He walked through the rooms, fond memories of his teenage years washing over him. This place was linked to the James women. Thanks to Tori's selflessness, Barbara wouldn't have to worry about her shop.

In the kitchen, he set the box on a counter lined with matching file organizers. The door to the porch stood wide-open. Strange.

Cade stepped through to the porch and found Tori about to brave the elements.

"You'll need a raincoat and boots."

Snatching her hand back, she spun and pressed her hand to her throat. Her skin was leached of color.

"What's wrong?"

"I heard something, so I came to investigate and saw someone out there." She pointed to the detached garage and the profuse bushes marching behind it and linking to Kenneth the tax man's property. "At least, I thought I did."

"Could it have been Kenneth?" He didn't like that the

man had studied Tori's movements. "Does he have a pet that might've escaped?"

He moved closer to her and looked through the screens. The view was obstructed by the relentless downpour.

"He has a cat, but I don't think he'd be inclined to pursue her through this."

"I'll check it out."

She sidestepped to block the door. "You don't have to do that. I'm more rattled than I realized, and my mind's probably playing tricks. It could've been a large dog. There's a black lab that roams the neighborhood every time his owners forget to latch the fence."

"Can I borrow an umbrella?"

She arched a brow. "Still stubborn, I see."

"We'll both feel better if I do this."

"Fine." She disappeared into the house and returned a minute later. He examined the oversize dog faces printed on the material.

He let out an exaggerated sigh. "Let's hope none of my buddies happen by."

Wind and rain battered his lower body. And it hindered his ability to look for clues. There weren't any discernible footprints. Nor was anyone lurking behind the structure. A stand of trees separated Tori's lot from the one behind hers. He couldn't detect movement in that person's yard. The garage itself was locked, the lone window intact.

Back inside, he wiped the mud from his shoes. "I didn't see anything or anyone suspicious."

"Good." A furrow dug between her brows, advertising her continued disquiet.

"Has Kenneth ever done anything to make you uncomfortable?"

She shook her head. "He's a little frazzled and absent-minded, but he's harmless."

"You don't find it odd that he knows your schedule?"

"Having nosy neighbors can actually be a good thing. Crime deterrents. Besides, I have an alarm system. We had one installed several years ago."

Cade propped the umbrella in the corner. "Do you know if sensors were installed in the windows?"

"On this level, they were."

Outside, there was a second set of stairs leading to the upper-level deck, which stretched the rear facade of the house—easy access to the entrance door and windows.

"You might want to consider installing them on the second floor, just to be safe."

She studied his face more closely. "You're worried. Why? Deputy Claxton wasn't."

"Maybe because I've experienced my fair share of violence."

"That's your world, not mine."

"Nothing wrong with staying proactive."

"That word again," she groaned. "The Marines' way of saying an ounce of caution is worth a pound of cure."

"Served me well over the years."

"There's a rational explanation for the car. I'm sure of it."

Inside the kitchen, Tori locked the door and checked it twice, a sign she wasn't as confident as she'd like him to think.

He noticed she held her wrist flush against her middle. "Did I do that?"

He'd shoved her to the ground with scarcely a thought to where she landed. He inched closer, curved his fingers around her arm and gingerly inspected it. "Looks swollen."

"It's a little sore," she murmured, easing free of his touch. "Nothing serious."

"I'm sorry. I reacted without thinking."

"You were trying to protect me."

"And wound up hurting you."

Her eyes darkened with unpleasant memories. That last scene in the local college library was seared into his mind. Cade hadn't known he could inflict such pain.

"Tori—"

"Here's the deposit bag," she exclaimed, snatching it from the dining table and heading for the front. "We should get going."

Cade followed at a more sedate pace. She wasn't ready to hear his apology. He'd been naive, thinking that one conversation could mend the rift between them. Friendship with Tori was probably out of reach, but he'd thought they could at least put the past to rest and be friendly acquaintances.

Tori insisted on walking with him to the bank at the end of the street, a brief distance made miserable by the continuing onslaught. But by the time they'd dropped off her deposit and completed their business at the hardware store, the rain had stopped and the gray clouds were starting to disperse. Tori's stomach growled as he was loading the new window.

"I heard that," he told her. "Why don't we stop at Red's on the way?"

She placed a bag of tools in the back seat. "I don't know."

"Surely you can't turn down a cheeseburger and fries." He came around to her side. "I'll throw in that ice cream cone I promised earlier."

"Spending time with you…pretending we're fine…" She bit her lip and took her time examining the parking lot.

His heart squeezed. "I get it."

"This can't be easy for you, either."

"I've come to accept that most things worth doing aren't easy." He gestured to the vehicle. "It's just a casual dinner."

The look she gave him indicated there wasn't anything casual about it. "We're both reasonable adults," she said at last. "No reason why we can't share a meal, I suppose."

"Exactly."

"But no personal talk and no stealing my fries."

"I don't make promises I can't keep," he quipped, thinking of past visits to the diner.

His conscience pricked him. Hadn't he promised to be there for her? To love and support her? To put her needs above his own?

Those were some of the most important promises a man could make to a woman, and he hadn't kept a single one.

God, please help me not to hurt her again. More than anything, I want to make amends. I want Tori's forgiveness.

Only then could they move beyond past mistakes and live in the same town with any sense of normalcy.

THREE

How had a normal, routine day turned into something out of a strange dream?

First her car went up in flames, then her apartment was damaged and now she was being yanked down memory lane against her will. When she'd agreed to eat with Cade, she hadn't factored in the power of nostalgia.

Here she was in what used to be their favorite booth, seated across a narrow stretch of silver-flecked Formica, with 1950s' songs belting from the jukebox. Nothing about this place had changed. Pictures of Elvis still hung on the walls. Cherry-red padded bar stools lined the bar. The smell of grease, fries and burgers mingled with chocolate malt.

She shouldn't have agreed to this.

I'm in trouble, Lord. I can't pretend my heart doesn't ache for the days when I could tell Cade anything. He was my closest, dearest friend. I've missed him.

She managed to order without sounding as if this blast of sentimentality was filling her with sadness. At least the young waitress was a new face, someone unfamiliar with their history. Because Sneads Ferry was situated right outside Camp Lejeune's back gate, it was a popular

spot for military personnel to live. People were continu-
ally moving in and out of the area.

"When are you going to tell your mom?"

"I don't know." She wished she could avoid it. "I'd like
to wait until after the party."

"I saw her last week at my parents' fish fry. She looks
better. Not having to worry about the day-to-day responsibilities of the shop has helped, but I get the feeling she
misses her customers."

"They miss her, too. Not a day goes by that someone
doesn't ask about her."

"She'll be ready to return eventually. Once that happens, will you look for a position at a local library or return to Tennessee?"

She shrugged. "I don't want to rush Mom. And now
that I'm here, I'm realizing how disconnected Jason and
I have become. I'd like to rebuild our relationship, but
he's resisting."

Tori couldn't determine if his aloofness was because
he was a teenager and it wasn't cool to hang out with
his older sister or if her absence had driven a wedge between them.

"Give him time," Cade said. "He'll get used to having you around."

Not if he enlisted, he wouldn't. She held her tongue.
Hadn't she implied they were capable of a peaceful dinner?

"Blue Suede Shoes" belted from the jukebox. The
short-order cook called out to one of the waitresses.
Through the plateglass window, she watched a happy
couple strolling hand in hand into the riverfront park. As
they passed, Tori spotted a man in a black baseball cap,
tattered jeans and boots, with a tattoo curled around his
biceps and forearm. A snake, maybe? His cap pulled low

over his sunglasses, he was standing beside a blue mail receptacle and staring straight at them. The moment he realized she'd seen him, he pivoted and cut a diagonal path through the park.

Tori dragged her gaze from the retreating stranger. Her imagination was leaping to irrational conclusions.

A plate of seasoned fries and a cheeseburger was set before her. The aroma of seared meat and smoky bacon teased her nose. Although Cade had ordered the same, he snagged one of her fries and popped it in his mouth, a boyish smile flashing.

"Try that again, Staff Sergeant, and you'll regret it." She made a show of pulling the plate closer to her.

At her use of his title, his brows shot up in silent question.

"It's on your collar." She brandished a fry toward the metal pins affixed to the sturdy material. "It should come as no surprise that my mom has kept me informed of your ascent through the ranks. I know that you're in charge of thirty-nine Marines and that you were hailed a hero during your last deployment."

Six months ago, her mom told her that Cade had been involved in an ambush and had saved someone. Tori had experienced nightmares for weeks afterward. Off and on through the years, she'd considered telling her mom to cease with the updates. They weren't a couple anymore. They didn't text or email. Didn't follow each other on social media. But she hadn't been able to cut off the flow of information. Because no matter how much time passed, she needed to know he was all right.

Cade fiddled with the straw in his milkshake, his mouth grim. "Kind of difficult to think of myself that way when we lost someone. I may have helped Corporal Faulkner, but I wasn't able to do anything to save William Poole. He was an outstanding Marine." The haunted look about his eyes troubled her. His fingers pressed into the beveled glass.

"Surely you don't blame yourself."

"Did I do what I thought was right at the time? Yes. I relied on my training and sheer instinct. Not everyone was satisfied with my performance, however. Two Marines in my platoon lodged complaints with our command, which led to an informal investigation into my actions."

"But you weren't found to be at fault."

"No."

Tori wanted to reach across and squeeze his hand. Offering him comfort used to be second nature.

"I thought we'd agreed to keep the conversation shallow and meaningless," she lightly chided.

"You're too easy to talk to. That hasn't changed."

Whatever else he might've said was lost by a foreign sound. A high-pitched ping. Glass splintering. A heavy *thwack*.

Then, for the second time in the span of a few hours, Cade was diving for her.

Screams rent the air. Another round whizzed into the diner.

Cade's focus narrowed to one thing—keeping Tori safe.

Familiar with the hail of gunfire, he'd tugged her to the space beneath the table and ordered the others to hunker down. Somewhere in the room, a woman sobbed. A baby's helpless cries prompted him to action.

He gripped her shoulders. "Stay here."

"Where are you going?" Her eyes were huge pools of dread.

"To see if I can spot the shooter before he decides to come inside."

"Are you armed?"

In answer, he lifted his pant leg and removed his Beretta Jetfire from the ankle holster. His larger weapon was at home in the safe, more suited to long-range targets. This one would have to do.

He twisted toward the kitchen area and hoped some of the employees had escaped through the rear exit. There was no evidence of blood, no anguished moans that typically accompanied wounds. *Lord Jesus, let us all survive this.*

Tori gasped. "Cade, your arm's bleeding."

The light was dim in the space beneath the table. He prodded the area and came away with bloodstained fingers. A needle-sharp sting registered through the rush of adrenaline. "Feels superficial."

Another bullet pierced the glass above them.

"I have to go."

Jaw locked, she gave a tight nod.

Cade inched farther onto the tiles and scanned the crowd. "Anyone hit?"

Those trapped beneath the tables in the middle stared at him in shock. In the far corner, an older man with a high-and-tight haircut—likely a retired Marine—lifted his shirt to reveal a pistol. "We're okay on this side."

Satisfied there were no wounds to tend, Cade darted toward the side door that led to an alley and trash dumpsters. If he could reach those dumpsters, he could use them as a buffer while searching for their assailant. Crouching low, he rushed outside. Oppressive heat mixed with eerie silence. The gravel beneath his shoes crunched. Blood singing through his veins brought back memories of Afghanistan and the kill-or-be-killed mind-set. Instead of Marines, he was protecting a diner full of civilians. And Tori.

Weapon drawn, he wedged into a slim crevice between the metal dumpster and brick building. The rain-dampened sidewalks were empty. Water droplets coating the playground equipment glittered in the waning sunlight. He squinted at the storefronts farther down, but the angle wasn't right.

Where are you?

Who are you?

Cade braced for further assault and prayed that Tori would stay put.

Was this a random act? Maybe a disgruntled former employee with an ax to grind?

An employee trained in sniper-like kills?

Doubtful.

In the back of his mind, he kept connecting this to the explosion earlier that day. He didn't want to. Tried to reject it. But he'd lived in Sneads Ferry all his life and couldn't remember a single incident like this one.

Sirens announced the approach of law enforcement. The gunman must've heard it, too, because there were no more shots fired. The first officer to arrive was an acquaintance of Cade's, sparing him the need to get on the ground until they figured out he wasn't involved. Cade sprinted over and, crouching behind the patrol car, told him everything he knew. Tori rushed into the street before they'd given the all clear.

Ignoring the officers' protests, she hurried to join Cade. He seized her hand and tugged her down. "You're not supposed to be out here," he growled.

"I remembered something. While we were waiting for our order, I saw a man. He was watching us."

The gut feeling he'd had solidified. Over her shoulder,

he studied the diner's facade. Tori turned to see what he was looking at. What scant color there was left in her face drained, and she lifted a trembling hand to clutch her neck.

"Cade…"

Only one of the plateglass windows had been blown out. Theirs.

"My car. It wasn't an accident, was it?" Her gaze swerved to his, begging him to refute her claim.

"We can't know that for sure—"

"Someone *shot* at us." She had to work to drag in air. "You told me not to ignore my instincts. I should've heeded your advice. Someone has been watching me since I returned. Waiting for an opportunity to…"

She didn't finish the sentence. Didn't have to.

They both knew that, had the timing of the car explosion been different, had the shooter's aim been a little more accurate, Tori would be dead already.

FOUR

"Why would someone target you?" Cade demanded. "Did something happen in Tennessee? Something you're afraid to share?"

His words doused her in cold shock.

Secrets were her former boyfriend's specialty. Patrick, with whom she'd shared a fun, low-key relationship, had turned out to be a white-collar criminal. His arrest and conviction hadn't shattered her heart so much as shaken her confidence in her ability to discern a person's true character.

Not about to share her humiliation with Cade, she said, "My life is ordinary."

His head sagged against the bumper. "Nothing about this is ordinary, Tori." He sighed.

Beneath his tattered sleeve, blood trickled down his biceps. She sidled closer, the hot pavement searing her bare knees, and reached for his wounded arm. "You need medical attention."

He shifted away. "It'll keep a while longer."

"I won't pass out." At his disbelieving stare, she said, "I'm not as squeamish as I used to be."

"You aren't going to swoon in my arms like a Jane Austen heroine?"

She was unable to banish the memory of her seventeenth birthday and the incident involving a rusty nail in her foot. He'd carried her half a mile to the nearest residence, called for an ambulance and refused to leave her side. He'd been her own personal hero. Well, she was older and wiser. More cynical? Or was it that her heart had been broken at eighteen and never fully repaired? Whatever the case, she didn't believe in heroes anymore. Exceptional romance belonged on library shelves.

Cade didn't seem inclined to reminisce further. His gun clutched in one hand, he scrutinized the area around the diner. She could picture him on the battlefield... focused, in command, lethal. Above all, willing to sacrifice his life for his men and his country. Hadn't she witnessed his bravery twice already? He'd put her safety first both times a threat arose. Tori's gaze sought out his injury, and her mind played out a deadlier scenario. If he'd been sitting in a different spot, if the bullet had drifted a few inches to the left, she wouldn't be here talking to him.

Tori angled her face away to hide the raw emotion coursing through her.

The minutes ticked by, the humidity suffocating, the wait almost unbearable. Where had the shooter gone? Was he watching them now? The *why* of this situation escaped her.

Deputy Claxton arrived and, after conferring with the North Topsail police, ushered them to a waiting ambulance. While a paramedic cleaned and stitched his wound, Cade related the evening's events, moment by moment. The deputy's attention switched to her. He must've come to the same conclusions they had, because his questions probed into her private life.

She twisted her hands together, wincing when her wrist protested. "I've dated off and on since college.

Nothing serious until Patrick. My relationship with him lasted a year and a half."

Deputy Claxton's pencil hovered above the paper. "Patrick's last name?"

"Livingston. We ended things last summer." Keenly aware of Cade's laser-like perusal, she was reluctant to add details.

The deputy wasn't having it. "Occupation? Current location?"

"He's, ah, in a correctional facility."

Cade's brows hit his hairline. "Tori—"

"Patrick embezzled funds from his company. I didn't find out until the news of his arrest hit social media."

The scowl on his face was at odds with the compassion filling his eyes. Unable to bear his pity, she dropped her gaze.

"Safe to say he isn't our shooter," Claxton said. "But that doesn't rule out the possibility he orchestrated it from behind bars. Would you say he was angry with you? Did he expect you to stick with him through thick and thin?"

"Not at all. Patrick regretted pulling my name into it. Not once did he ask me to stay. We didn't have that kind of relationship."

While she hadn't wanted to dwell on it at the time, their connection had been shallow. Nothing like what she'd had with Cade.

More scribbling. "Did you have any fractious relationships in your former workplace? Jealous coworkers? Friendships that soured?"

"I can't think of a single person who'd want to hurt me."

She made the mistake of glancing at Cade, whose eyes burned with righteous determination. "Think harder. There must be *someone*." He paid no heed as the paramedic snipped off the thread. "You need to make a list of acquaintances, college buddies, professors—"

"I graduated years ago."

"Write down every single employee at that library you used to work at, from the cleaning crew to the folks behind the check-in desk." He counted on his fingers. "If you don't know their names, we'll get them from Human Resources."

"How about you settle down and let me do my job, son." Deputy Claxton shot Cade a dry look. To Tori, he said, "Make the list. I'll be inputting the car explosion into the state database to see if there have been similar crimes."

"You got the report back?" Cade asked.

"Our guys aren't finished with the wreckage."

"But you're assuming it was an intentional act."

Before he could answer, another deputy walked over to deliver the news that they'd scoured the area. The perp was in the wind. They planned to canvas the neighborhood and conduct interviews. There was a chance someone other than Tori saw him and could give them valuable information.

Cade studied the buildings around them. "No traffic cameras, but there could be private security cameras."

"We'll consult the individual businesses," Claxon said. He left with a promise to contact her.

While Cade was being patched up, he caught the attention of a second paramedic and insisted Tori's wrist be examined. As expected, it was a slight sprain. She was testing out the snug wrap when she noticed a pair of young men in heated conversation with an officer. She hurried over.

The lanky blond one spotted her and frowned, his gaze on her wrist. "That's my sister."

The officer twisted around and, seeing her, allowed them to pass. She wasn't surprised to see her brother with his new friend, a shy but pleasant young man whom he'd met at the gym.

"Hello, Heath," she greeted the redhead before turning to her brother. "Jason, what are you doing here? I thought you were working tonight."

"Switched shifts with Billy, so I don't go in until eleven. Heath and I were headed to Red's to meet up with a few buddies."

He reached up to smooth his hair, only to come up empty. Like her, he was still adjusting to his altered appearance. Without his wavy blond locks, he looked less like the surfer he was and more like a Marine. *He's eighteen. No longer the adoring little brother you left behind.*

"What happened?"

A female officer speaking into her radio passed by. Jason watched the hushed activity around them, especially the subdued customers trickling out of the diner and waitresses huddled around the splintered window. Their faces were ravaged by the horror they'd endured.

"There was a shooting."

Behind his glasses, Heath's puppy-dog eyes filled with disbelief. "In Sneads Ferry?"

"Hard to accept, I know," she agreed, wondering how she was going to tell Jason about the car and their suspicions.

"Was anyone hurt?" Jason asked.

"A bullet grazed Cade's arm, but he's going to be okay."

Heath's gaze shifted beyond Tori, and he snapped to attention. "Good evening, Staff Sergeant."

She turned to see Cade approaching. He inclined his head. "Lance Corporal Polanski."

"You two know each other?"

"Staff Sergeant McMann is my platoon leader," Heath explained.

"Fortunate for you," Jason said, his admiration plain.

When Tori transferred to a university in Knoxville, she got busy carving out a new life for herself. Meanwhile, Cade took Jason under his wing. She was grateful to a point. Cade was a good role model. But she couldn't help but be a tad jealous of their close bond.

"Why would someone want to shoot up Red's?" Jason mused.

Tori intercepted Cade's probing glance. She reached for the ring on her right hand and twisted the silver dolphin. "We have reason to believe the shooter was after me."

Deep grooves distorted his forehead. "What?"

Beside him, Heath paled, the smattering of freckles on his nose stark against his skin. "Why would you assume such a thing?"

"Earlier this evening, my car exploded. Right around the time I usually drive to the bank with the shop's earnings."

"I don't understand." Jason pinched the bridge of his nose. "Why would someone target you? You're a *librarian*." He said it like it was the most mundane job in the world.

Cade shifted closer to Tori, determination gripping his features. "That's what we're going to figure out."

"You can't stay in the apartment," Jason said. "This guy knows where you live."

"I can't abandon the shop. It's Mom's baby. Besides, there will be deputies parked outside." For tonight only. They simply didn't have the manpower to guard her around the clock indefinitely. But she didn't tell her brother that. "Maybe he'll come back tonight and they'll snag him."

"And what if he takes them by surprise and manages to get to you?"

The depth of her brother's concern surprised her. She'd started to think he resented her to the point of dislike.

"I'm staying, too." Cade's tone brooked no argument—one she suspected he used on his junior Marines.

"The commanding officer routine doesn't work on me," she responded.

"I'm not an officer. No college degree, remember? I'm a grunt, like Heath here."

"That's beside the point. You're not staying."

"Accept his help, sis." Jason's blue eyes were serious. "I'd be there if I didn't have to work."

"I'll sleep downstairs. If anyone breaches the house, I'll know about it."

His goal had been to deal with the past so they could move on with their lives. But moving on wasn't going to happen as soon as they'd hoped, not with him acting as her protector. And while spending time with him would prove a minefield of emotional traps, Tori couldn't bring herself to face her unknown enemy alone.

Cade placed his weapon on the kitchen counter as Tori entered the room with a pillow and an armful of blankets. Her gaze fell on the gun and the shadows in her eyes deepened. She'd swapped her breezy summer dress for a blue pajama pant set that looked like something from the fifties.

She gestured to the military-issue sleeping bag rolled out on the linoleum. "That's not going to be comfortable."

"Compared to some of the spots I've slept in, this is

a luxury. No sand fleas or other pests. Central heat and air. Indoor plumbing."

She looked as if she'd like to question him, but refrained. He took the blankets from her and set them on one of the dining chairs. The day's events were taking their toll. He'd been at the base by 0500 hours for a strenuous round of PT—a five-mile hump carrying fifty pounds of gear through the woods. The stores of adrenaline that had carried him through the explosion and shooting were depleted. Getting winged hadn't helped matters.

But he couldn't sleep. Not even with two cruisers parked outside, one in the driveway and the other on the curb. Tori's life was being threatened, and he'd do anything to ensure her safety.

He nodded to the only photo in the room, a casual shot of a champagne-colored poodle with big amber eyes lounging on Tori's lap. "Who's that?"

"Beatrice. Bee for short."

"After your favorite Beverly Cleary character, right?"

"Beezus and Ramona. I still have that book." Looking surprised he'd remembered, she picked up the frame. "I wish Bee was still around." Sadness tinted her tone.

"What happened?"

"Bloat. I didn't catch the signs fast enough."

"I'm sorry." Tori had a big heart for animals. Over the years, the James family had adopted an assortment of dogs, birds and even a couple of lizards. No cats, though, because Barbara was allergic.

Cade's curiosity about her life in Tennessee strained to the breaking point. His mom hadn't shared specifics, like what kind of place she'd lived in or what she'd done for fun. She certainly hadn't mentioned that lousy excuse for an ex-boyfriend.

"She obviously adored you. Looks like she's smiling."

A bittersweet smile curved her lips. "For the short while we were together, we relished each other's company."

"Will you ever get another one?"

She replaced the frame. "I was considering it before I decided to come home. With my life in limbo, adopting doesn't make sense right now."

"So you love on your customers' pets instead."

"Yeah, that about sums it up." She seemed very much alone, and he hated that. "If you don't need anything else, I'm going to call my mom."

"I'm good."

"Good night, Cade."

"Good night."

He listened to her retreating footsteps and waited for the soft click of the upstairs door. Then he picked up the picture frame and stared at the image, his insides in turmoil. When he'd woken up that morning, he couldn't have imagined he'd become Tori's bodyguard by the end of the day.

The attempts on her life had blown his original plan to bits. He'd had an idea of how things were supposed to go. He'd apologize. She'd forgive him and possibly admit she'd been wrong about some things, too. They'd discuss inane details of their post-engagement lives, shake hands and part ways with clear consciences. He'd been positive they could coexist with little interaction.

That was before the explosion. Before a sniper shot up a diner trying to end her life. His blood ran cold each time he replayed the chaos, the stark fear in her eyes. He wouldn't abandon her. He'd just have to keep in mind that what they'd had was over. They weren't going to get a second chance. Tori had no real place in his life anymore.

FIVE

"Miss James?" Deputy Clark stood on the main porch the next morning. "There's a woman here who says she has a delivery of cookies?"

Peeking over his shoulder, Tori recognized the brunette waiting outside the gate. "Oh, that's Felicia Ortiz. She has a batch of dog treats for me."

The deputy summoned her with a flick of his fingers and then returned to his vehicle. The other deputy had left about fifteen minutes prior, leaving Clark alone until later this afternoon. Cade had left before breakfast to go home and shower and change.

Unwilling to leave the safety of the house, Tori waited inside the foyer. "Felicia, I forgot to tell you we're closed today."

After discussing the issue with her mom last night, they'd decided it was safer for Tori and their customers to close.

A large plastic box in her hands, Felicia entered the house and paused by the wall of paintings depicting silly dog faces. "I heard about your car. Is that why the police are here? Do they think you're in some sort of danger?"

Explaining her predicament to her mother had been a challenge. Tori wasn't ready to attempt it with Felicia, someone she barely knew. "Their presence is merely a precaution. Car explosions are few and far between in Sneads Ferry. The neighbors are on edge. I figured business would be slow today."

"The whole town's rattled after what happened at the diner." Felicia's dark eyes brimmed with incredulity. "Two major news stories in one day. Must be a record."

"It is unusual," Tori agreed. Felicia didn't appear to know about Tori's involvement, which was a relief.

"Will you have a problem getting a replacement vehicle?"

"I've spoken to my insurance company, and they've offered to provide a rental until I can shop for one."

Car shopping wasn't on her list of fun tasks. Not like shoe shopping. But after yesterday, she'd be grateful for a chance to do mundane chores without the threat of another attempt on her life dogging her steps.

Leaving her half-finished coffee on the entry table, she led the way to the middle of the parlor. "What do we have today? In her email, Maria indicated she was thinking about doing some Fourth-of-July-inspired treats."

Felicia removed the lid, revealing an assortment of frosted shapes. "She's going to wait until the end of the month, closer to the holiday."

"These are pretty. I like the strawberry ones."

"Maria's schnauzer does, too. Polly stole three of them before I noticed."

Tori smiled. "How are Maria and the baby?"

Their supplier for more than a year, Maria had given birth prematurely last month. Her cousin, Felicia, had stepped in to help whenever she wasn't on duty. The Marine sergeant was polite to a fault and exuded an air of competence.

"They're both great." She fished a small card from her

back pocket. "Maria sent a thank-you card to your mom. She adores the baby blanket."

"I'll be sure to pass it along."

They worked together on the display. Tori placed the older treats in a bag in order to give Felicia space to set out the fresh ones.

"These are going to the shelter on Franklin Street, right?"

Felicia nodded, her espresso-colored hair rippling over her shoulders. When in uniform, she wore it in a tight bun. The loose style softened her hard edges. "That's right. The workers appreciate your generosity since the budget won't allow for extras like this." She cast Tori a side-glance. "I hope closing today won't put too much of a dent in sales."

"We can handle a day here and there."

Worry threatened to choke her. What if the police couldn't identify this guy? She couldn't become a permanent hermit, afraid to step outside her house. Not to mention the financial impact on her mother's shop if they had to keep it closed indefinitely.

Her mom had been terribly upset that her daughter's life was in jeopardy, but she'd clung to her faith and reminded Tori of God's promises.

Fear not, for I am with you; be not dismayed, for I am your God. I will strengthen you.

Yes, I will help you, I will uphold you with My righteous right hand.

Whoever this madman was, he'd make a mistake eventually.

Hopefully before he completed his mission. A shudder shimmied through her.

Another knock on the door sent her pulse racing. "Excuse me for a minute."

Deputy Clark was at the door again, this time with an employee of the alarm company she'd contacted last night. After reassuring the deputy, she let the man inside. About midtwenties, he had the appearance of a Marine. His blond hair was cut to regulation, and peeking from his long-sleeved shirt was what looked like an eagle, globe and anchor tattoo. Definitely Marine. Maybe he had a side job. Or he'd been discharged and stuck around the area.

"I'm Brandon." His gray eyes roamed the merchandise along the hallway before snagging on Felicia, who was still in the parlor. "You're wanting to wire the windows on the second floor, is that right?"

"Yes. Thank you for coming out on short notice."

"No problem, ma'am. We had a cancelation, so we were able to fit you in." He held a toolbox in one hand, a clipboard in the other.

"Give me a moment." Leaving him in the foyer, she hurried to the cash register and retrieved the envelope containing Maria's check. "Would you mind taking this to your cousin?"

"I'll drop it off after I stop at the shelter." She put the envelope inside her now-empty plastic container and then grabbed the bag of treats. "Maria or I will contact you midweek to see if you want another batch next weekend."

"Thanks, Felicia."

They walked together to the door. Tori watched her leave through the garden and wave to the deputy, who was inside his cruiser.

She almost called her back. Brandon's presence behind her put her on edge. Before yesterday, she wouldn't have felt uneasy being alone with a stranger. Being a target had changed her perceptions.

He's here at my request, she reminded herself. *An employee of a reputable company.*

Turning, she pasted on a smile. "It's this way."

"Don't forget your coffee."

"Right." With mug in hand, she ascended first.

Every step of the way, she felt his gaze boring into her back. She found herself wishing Cade was there with her, which was irritating. She'd lived on her own for many years and managed just fine.

Inside the apartment, she gave him a quick tour of the rooms. A faint scent of cigarette smoke clung to his clothes, competing with his aftershave. His manner was polite, but his eyes followed her in a way that made her uncomfortable.

She covered her nervousness by sipping on her coffee, which tasted more bitter than usual.

"I'll start in your bedroom," he said.

"I'll stay out of your way."

Tori drained the mug and ventured past the dining table and open kitchen to the living area. The cream walls were devoid of pictures, and there was a stack of cardboard boxes in the corner waiting to be unpacked. The apartment wasn't completely organized yet, but the books in the built-in shelves on either side of the fireplace and decorative pillows on the sage sofa made it feel like home. This was her sanctuary. Her safe space.

The memory of the explosion and the savageness of the flames mocked her. She didn't *feel* safe.

Going to the window overlooking the street, she watched a pair of bicyclists navigate the sidewalk. Over at the bed-and-breakfast, a young man and woman unloaded their suitcases. Newlyweds? The area got a lot of those, eager to honeymoon at the beach.

Like yesterday, the sun was obscured by clouds, leaving the day cooler than usual and gloomy. Suddenly light-headed, she gripped the windowsill and waited for the moment to pass. Skipping breakfast was catching up with her.

Her phone buzzed. The screen indicated it was Angela, a dear friend Tori had made during sophomore year in high school. Reconnecting with her this past month had been a joy.

"Why am I getting secondhand accounts of your adventures from the nurses on my floor?" Angela demanded when Tori answered.

"What exactly did you hear?"

"Nancy's sister lives on your street. She said your car is toast."

"Sounds about right."

"There's also a photograph of the damaged diner circulating on the local news sites. I recognized you in the background, conversing with law enforcement. I learned of the shooting last night, but I had no idea you were there." A thread of uncertainty laced her voice. "Are you okay? I'm assuming you would've let me know if you'd gotten hurt."

"I have a sprained wrist. Very minor. I would've called you, but everything happened so fast…" She trailed off, the scene in the booth replaying in vivid detail. One minute she'd been having a meal with Cade, the next she'd been dodging bullets.

"Tori?"

"I was the target," she blurted.

Stunned silence stretched over the line. "What did you say?"

"The shooter was aiming for me. I'm positive I spotted him in the park across the street before it happened."

"But the news article didn't mention a motive or list the names of people in the diner."

"The sheriff's office is keeping certain information out of the news for now." Tori hoped her name stayed out of it. Reporters hounding her night and day would be a major headache. Not to mention they might dig into her past and discover her ties to Patrick. The Canine Companion didn't need that kind of press.

"I'm sorry you're dealing with this." She sighed. "Are you at the shop? I'll come over and keep you company."

She pressed her hand to her nape, surprised to find it damp. "That's not a good idea, Ang. Too dangerous. I have police protection for now. And Cade slept in the shop overnight. He'll be back soon."

The beat of silence was telling. "You're with Mr. America?"

Tori hadn't heard that old nickname in a long while. Angela had dubbed him Mr. America because he'd epitomized what every young man would want for themselves—the popular student who was beloved by students and teachers alike. Very few people knew he had to work harder than most others to achieve decent grades or that his family life didn't resemble a fairy tale.

"How are you holding up?"

Tori gripped the phone more tightly. "I'm managing to hold it together." Barely.

"Oh, Tori." She whistled low, and Tori could picture the worry in her ebony eyes. Angela had been a shoulder to cry on throughout Tori and Cade's friendship-to-romance saga. And while the optimistic nurse liked Cade, she understood how difficult it would be for Tori to be around him again.

"Do you have any idea who's behind this?"

Her stomach spasmed. Woozy, she pressed her forehead to the cool glass.

"Tori?"

"There's no one."

"No creepy men stalking you at the shop?"

"We have our share of unique patrons, but they're harmless."

"What about in your neighborhood?"

"The neighbors are nice, regular people."

"Some of the most infamous psychopaths appeared to be nice, regular people."

Confusion welling up, frustration on its heels, she tried to recall if there'd been anyone acting strangely. This area was an eclectic mix of restored homes, thriving businesses and pockets of sketchy behavior.

"My mom hasn't ever indicated she felt unsafe. I wouldn't have taken the apartment if either of us had reservations."

"I'm simply trying to consider all the angles."

"You sound like Cade."

"I'm worried for you."

"Pray for me," she murmured. "Pray this guy is caught before the day is out."

"You got it."

She ended the conversation with a promise to keep her friend updated.

She was debating whether or not to get a snack now or wait until lunch when the cruiser door swung open and the deputy got out. He was speaking into his radio and surveying the area between her house and Kenneth's. With a glance at her front door, he left his vehicle and rushed out of sight.

Tori's skin flushed hot. Had someone been lurking

where they shouldn't be and a neighbor reported it? Her unknown enemy about to strike?

At the creak of a floorboard directly behind her, she whirled around and came face-to-face with the alarm company employee.

"Brandon," she gasped, reaching for the nearest chair to steady herself. The room swung crazily. Her heart strained in her chest. What was wrong with her? "I—I didn't hear you. Do you need something?"

"As a matter of fact, I do need something." He stalked closer, his eyes hard and flat. The veins in his neck bulged. "You."

Horror pulsed through her. This couldn't be her enemy. He looked like a regular guy, not a killer. She didn't *know* him. Why would he want to hurt her?

Her fingers dug into the cushions as nausea attacked. "Y-you work for the alarm company. How—"

He kept coming. The fact that he was letting her see his face registered, making her limbs quake. He didn't plan on leaving her alive.

"Technology is a valuable tool if you know how to use it," he said calmly. "You let me in your home, Tori. Your worst and last mistake."

She sucked in a breath. Brandon lunged for her. Covered her mouth with his hand. Trying to get free took immense effort. Her limbs felt weighted in cement.

Remembering what she'd learned during a self-defense class in college, she kneed him in the groin. Or tried to.

His satisfied laugh sent a riot of goose bumps over her flesh. "You're not feeling quite yourself, are you, Tori?"

The nausea intensified. Had he drugged her?

Then she remembered. The coffee. Unattended while she got Felicia's check.

His arm came around her waist, locking her against

him in a terrible embrace. She clawed at his hand, but to no avail. Black dots danced before her eyes.

"No use fighting it," he murmured, his cheek pressed to her temple. "Just let the darkness swallow you."

Tori moaned deep in her throat, angry at her helplessness. Her thoughts were like helium balloons, slipping away one by one.

Cade. She hadn't gotten a chance to apologize to Cade.

That, more than anything, made her want to weep.

Against her will, her internal urge to fight was snuffed out, and she slipped into unconsciousness.

Cade parked his Jeep in Tori's driveway, confused as to why there was only one deputy on guard and why that deputy's vehicle was empty.

Scoping out the area around the garage and Kenneth's side yard, he entered the gated area and pounded on the front door. Nothing stirred inside. He tried the knob. Locked.

He punched in her cell number and paced the length of the porch. When it went to voice mail, he jogged around the side of the house, intent on using the outside stairs. Surely she would've texted him if she'd decided to go somewhere. He'd promised to come back as soon as he'd showered and changed. Even while off duty, a Marine was required to be clean-shaven.

He mounted the wooden stairs and rapped on the door. There were no signs of movement through the windows.

He tried her cell again. A muted ring came from somewhere inside the apartment. If she was able to, she would've picked up.

A heavy sense of dread invaded him. Why had the deputy abandoned his post? And where was Tori?

Pivoting, he crossed to the deck railing. Green lawn

stretched to trees and knee-high grass. A brook dissected her property with that of her neighbor's behind her. To the right was a vacant, thickly wooded lot. Barbara had said that vagrants sometimes used the lot as a spot to camp. They didn't get away with it for long, since the residents on that street kept a sharp eye out.

He scanned the entire lot and didn't at first notice anything out of place. Then a flash of color in the midst of the monotonous greens and browns. Holding back a shout, he leaned over the railing as far as he dared. It looked like a man with a woman tossed over his shoulder. The flash of color he'd glimpsed was pale blond hair.

Tori.

He flew down the stairs and raced across the lawn, toward the trees. *Please, God. Please let her be okay. Please don't let him take her.*

The stranger must've heard his boots splashing in the brook, because he whipped around to track the sounds. Beneath the bill of his baseball hat, his eyes widened and then narrowed.

The sight of Tori's limp body filled Cade with desperate rage.

"Let her go," he growled, pushing his legs faster.

"Stop! Police!"

Coming from the direction of Kenneth's, Deputy Clark joined the chase, his weapon drawn.

The man ignored the deputy's order and continued his bid for escape. When he emerged onto the street, yards from what had to be the getaway car, fear seized Cade. The perp had a solid head start and didn't seem to be letting the extra weight slow him down.

In the next heartbeat, he had the side door open.

They weren't going to reach her in time.

Sliding to a stop, Cade removed his weapon and, releasing the safety, shot out the taillight. Far enough away from Tori that she wouldn't be in danger of being hit by a ricochet bullet, but close enough to serve as a warning to the perp.

Clark was catching up. "Hold your fire, Staff Sergeant."

The stranger hesitated for a fraction of a second. Then he dumped Tori in the grass and dashed around the front, hopped inside and peeled out.

Cade ran to her side and fell to his knees, gently turned her onto her back and smoothed the hair from her face. The paleness of her lips and skin frightened him, but she was warm and breathing.

She was alive.

Thank You, Jesus.

"Tori? Wake up, sweetheart. Talk to me."

There was zero indication she'd heard him. Whatever that man had done to her had knocked her out cold.

"We need an ambulance," he ground out. "Now."

The deputy joined them. "On their way. In the meantime, I'll need your weapon."

"Yes, sir."

He handed the small Jetfire over, not taking his eyes from Tori.

"I don't condone what you did," he said, "but your actions saved her life."

"Where were you?" he demanded, giving voice to the question nagging him. Why hadn't Clark stayed at his post?

"Someone called in a tip about an intruder a few doors down, drawing me away from my vehicle."

He dragged his gaze away from Tori's motionless form. "Did you find anything?"

"No. Either someone really did see the perp wandering the neighborhood—"

"Or it was the perp who called, deliberately leaving Tori alone and vulnerable to attack."

SIX

An incessant beeping roused Tori. The ache in her head begged it to stop.

She blinked against the harsh light overhead. What was that stinging sensation in the back of her hand?

Memories cascaded into her mind, one after the other. That man. Brandon. He'd drugged her.

An acrid taste coated her mouth, and her stomach lurched. What else had he done?

A man's hand engulfed hers. "You're at the hospital, Tori. You're going to be okay."

"Cade." Fear's tentacles eased its grip.

She felt him shift, and the light went out. "The nurse said you might have a headache. That better?"

She forced her eyes open. They were in a nondescript hospital room lit only by sunlight bleeding through the blinds. An IV tube was connected to her hand, which explained the discomfort.

Cade had pulled a chair as close as possible. While his words had exuded confidence, his eyes told another story. He couldn't hide his turmoil.

"Tell me what happened," she said, holding on to his hand as though it was a lifeline. His touch comforted her. Strengthened her.

"When I got to your place, the cruiser was empty. I didn't get a response from the main floor, so I went around to the apartment. I heard your phone ringing inside. That's when I figured out something was wrong. Then I saw a man carrying you through the vacant lot." A muscle ticked in his jaw. "Deputy Clark and I got close enough to force him to leave you behind."

Tori squeezed her eyes shut to keep the tears from escaping. A prayer of gratitude winged upward. She didn't want to think about where she'd be right now if God hadn't sent help.

Cade's fingers stroked her cheek. "I won't leave you again, Tori. I promise."

Battling to maintain her composure, she met his intense gaze. "This isn't your fault. Brandon got to me because I was naive."

Like she'd been with Patrick. Accepting the man at face value, unaware of the complications underneath the surface.

"His name is Brandon? Did he give you a last name?"

"Probably not his real name. And no, he didn't. He said he was with the alarm company. Somehow, he knew I'd requested the work on the windows. He was wearing an official-looking uniform."

Picturing his face, those insidious gray eyes and sneering mouth, made her break out in a cold sweat. Cade got up and retrieved a non-caffeinated soda and pack of crackers from the sink counter. He used the buttons to ease her bed into a sitting position and popped the lid. She sipped greedily, thirstier than she'd realized.

"What happened once he was inside?"

"We went upstairs and I showed him the layout of the apartment. He started in my room." She licked her dry, cracked lips. "I was in the living room when I started to feel strange. When he confronted me, I realized he'd dumped something in my coffee. I left it unattended for a few minutes."

Cade looked ill. "What then?"

"He grabbed me. Kept me from screaming." She wouldn't soon dispel the sensation of his breath on her neck, his arms imprisoning her. "I tried to summon the strength to get free, but I was so weak."

"It was the drug, Tori."

"I can't remember anything else. It's a blank."

Cade began to pace. "An anonymous caller lured Deputy Clark away with a report of a prowler a couple of houses down. He didn't find anything suspicious. At this time, we can't confirm whether or not it was a ploy."

"What if Brandon's not working alone?"

"I don't care if there's an entire regiment after you." He gritted his teeth, his eyes turning fierce. "No one's going to hurt you again, because they won't be allowed to come near you."

"You've already gotten shot because of me. I can't let you continue to put yourself in danger. Besides, you can't babysit me every minute of the day."

"That's where you're wrong."

Cade wasn't going anywhere. Not willingly, anyway.

"I have leave saved up. I'll use it all if I have to."

"Cade, no. I can't let you do that—"

"Already done." He'd made the call and asked for a two-week vacation. Fortunately, his command had agreed despite the short notice. The paperwork would be ready on Monday for him to sign. "You're stuck with me."

She bent her head, her tousled blond locks slipping forward to skim her jaws. "I've always been able to count on you," she said softly. "But it's been a long time since we were close."

He resumed his seat. Avoiding the IV, he splayed his fingers atop her forearm. "That doesn't mean you stopped being important to me."

Putting her fingertips to her lips, she blinked away the moisture and pretended to be engrossed in the informational posters on the wall.

"I owe you an apology, Victoria."

That got her attention. He only called her by her full name when things were serious. Like when he'd kissed her for the first time. And when he'd proposed.

"I've been meaning to since you got home, but then bullets started flying and I got distracted."

"You already apologized in your letters."

He sat up straighter. "You read those?"

"I considered answering but couldn't find the right words. And then you stopped writing."

"That's because I saw how happy you were with your friends, and I couldn't ruin the new life you'd built."

Beneath his hand, she shifted her arm closer to her body. "What do you mean you *saw* me?"

He let go. "After graduating boot camp, I drove to Knoxville." He remembered that trip like it happened yesterday. Nervous to the point of being sick, he'd offered up desperate prayers with each passing mile. "Your mom told me which dorm you were in."

"She never mentioned it to me."

"I asked her not to."

Confusion swirled in the green depths. "Why?"

"I hurt you. Made you miserable. Drove you from North Carolina and your family." He shook his head. "Seeing you that day, I made the choice to accept your original decision."

He'd often wondered if he'd made the right one. It wasn't his habit to give up on something he believed in. And he'd believed in them.

"I should've handled things differently," he said. "I should've discussed my desire to enlist with you before walking into that recruiter's office."

"Even if you had, we would've still been at an impasse." Sadness marked her features. "I'm not military-wife material."

He disagreed. Tori was resilient, independent and loyal, crucial traits that would aid in the success of a military marriage. But he wasn't going to argue the matter. He'd developed a somewhat wary view of married life himself, thanks to the breakup of his close friend Brett's marriage and the struggles some of the younger married men endured.

Someone knocked and Tori flinched. Cade stationed himself between her and the door. Only when he recognized Angela Reagan, their former classmate and a close friend of Tori's, did he let himself relax.

"Cade." If she was surprised to see him there, she didn't show it. She lifted a bouquet wrapped in plastic. "I come bearing gifts."

Stepping aside, he watched as the women hugged.

Tori buried her nose in the pastel blooms. "These are beautiful, Ang."

"I thought they might cheer you up." Her thick black braid swinging between her shoulder blades, she perused the information written in marker on the board across from the bed. "The blood tests confirmed what we suspected. It was GHB, or liquid ecstasy. Odorless. Colorless. Fast acting."

Fury over what she'd endured flushed through him

again. Her attacker had been bold enough to walk right through her front door. And confident of his success.

But what were his motives? Why risk moving her to another location?

Another visitor arrived then. Dr. Marcellus Beaumont, a highly respected surgeon in his early thirties who'd transferred to North Carolina from Southern Florida. Cade hadn't met the gentleman, but he'd read about him in the newspaper when he'd first arrived. He'd also seen him with Angela at area restaurants. They'd looked cozy together.

"Marcellus, I thought you were in surgery for several more hours." Angela slipped her arm through his, and the overhead fluorescent light bounced off the diamond sparkler on her finger. Ah, so it was serious.

"We had to postpone. My patient failed to stop his blood thinner as instructed." Marcellus addressed Tori. "Are they taking adequate care of you down here?"

"They've been nothing but efficient and kind."

"I'm glad to hear it." He turned to Cade with an outstretched hand. His dark eyes spoke of keen intelligence and compassion. "You must be Staff Sergeant McMann. Angela mentioned the three of you attended high school together."

"Nice to meet you." Cade shook his hand, glancing between the doctor and nurse. "I see congratulations are in order."

"Thank you." The surge of pride and contentment in Marcellus's expression belied his serious demeanor. "I'm a fortunate man."

Angela's grin stretched from ear to ear. "You say that now," she teased. "Wait until we've been married six months and you get tired of eating sandwiches and canned soup."

"I was aware of your aversion to the kitchen when I proposed. If you'll see to the laundry, I'll see to the meals."

"It's a deal."

Cade used to daydream about married life with Tori. The couple's banter reawakened slumbering wishes. Impossible dreams of spending every day and night with the woman he'd loved. Building a life together. A family. Stringing memories together to last forever.

"When's the big day?" he asked, refocusing on what was real, not fantasy.

"October," Angela gushed. "You're invited, of course."

Marcellus nodded. "Our engagement party is coming up. You're welcome to join us."

"You can't say no to a night of good food and music." Angela's enthusiasm dimmed. "Tori, you're still coming, right?"

"I don't know, Ang."

"You're in the wedding party. This is a chance to celebrate. To let loose and be silly. Plus, you'll get to know the other bridesmaids better."

Unhappiness tugged at her mouth. Studiously avoiding Cade's gaze, she said, "I'll do my best to be there."

After the couple left, he couldn't help cautioning her. "You're aware that your ability to attend rides on whether or not we've caught this guy."

She nodded somberly. "I couldn't bring myself to disappoint her."

Angela's and Tori's disappointment he could handle. What he couldn't stomach was the prospect of almost losing Tori again to this lowlife. Deputy Claxton interrupted them, as unflappable as ever.

"Here's what we know," he said, not bothering with small talk. "Clark got a partial plate on the perp's Mustang. That will take a while to run down. We contacted the alarm company, and they confirmed that no one matching Brandon's description works for them. They also said their guy logged your address at twenty past ten but wasn't heard from again. Deputy Hanson located the company van at the far end of your street and found the real employee—a Terrence Grayson—trussed and gagged in the back. And he was missing his uniform shirt and tool kit. We're interviewing him now."

Tori turned the soda can in an endless circle. "I assumed Brandon was current or former military. He had the haircut, the stance and a Marine tattoo."

Claxton notated her description in his pad. "You mentioned seeing a man at the park right before the shooting. He had a tattoo, as well. Do you have reason to believe it's the same man?"

"I don't know. He was wearing a long-sleeved shirt this time. And I didn't get a good look at the first guy's face."

"The shell casings we found belonged to an AR-15."

"A weapon military personnel are familiar with," Cade said.

"Miss James, we need to do a check of your person and see if we can find evidence of his DNA."

"I remember struggling with him. I might've scratched him, but I'm not sure."

"We'll also be sending in a sketch artist."

She pulled the thin sheet up to cover where the tubing was attached to her hand. "Can we make it quick? Because I don't plan on hanging around here all day."

Claxton shot Cade a quizzical look before replacing his pad in his pocket. "I'll see what I can do."

Cade moved to the end of her bed. She spoke before he could.

"I'm fine. Well, not fine, but I can recuperate at home." She caught herself, her brows crashing together. "I can't go home, can I?"

"The police are probably still there, searching for prints or hair or anything else the attacker left behind."

"He's arrogant, not stupid. I think he'll crawl into a hole for a while. In the meantime, I'll have to stay in a hotel. I won't endanger my mom or Angela."

The idea didn't sit well with Cade. "Stay with me."

Refusal immediately brewed on her lips.

"You'll have the upstairs to yourself. I'll sleep on the living room couch." He considered offering Jason a room, too, but he didn't need to be involved.

"I don't want to endanger you, either."

"I'm trained to handle untenable situations. I have an excellent alarm system, complete with video surveillance. I'd be better able to protect you in my own home than in a hotel."

"I didn't ask you to be my bodyguard. If something terrible happened to you, I'd blame myself."

"I can't walk away, Tori. Please don't ask me to."

SEVEN

Tori couldn't manage to do what she knew was best for Cade. She couldn't tell him to leave her alone. That's how she found herself in his home that afternoon.

Cade had ushered her through the garage and straight to the living room couch, where he'd insisted she stay. She didn't have the energy to defy him. Her weariness was bone-deep, the result of operating on too much adrenaline in a short period. Or maybe it was the drug's lingering effects. Her mind wasn't sluggish, however. Couldn't be when she was seeing her ex-fiancé's home for the first time.

A new construction two-story, it had a stone-and-wood siding exterior that lent it a rustic feel. Inside, there were gleaming hardwood floors and high ceilings. Landscape portraits of seaside scenes brought punches of color to the neutral walls and furniture. Lamps placed around the room gave it a cozy glow, while conch shells, starfish and sculptures of seabirds were whimsical nods to the nearby ocean.

He set a cup of peppermint tea on the coffee table and, seeing her studying the room, grimaced. "I picked out the furniture. The decorations were Mom's doing."

He handed her a mug sporting the eagle-globe-and-anchor symbol and settled onto the couch's opposite end.

"It's serene," she said. "And comfortable."

"It's a magazine spread," he laughed. "And not the kind I actually buy."

"Why don't you change it?"

"I'm renting the house from a family stationed in Okinawa. Once I get around to buying my own place, I'll put my stamp on it."

He tapped the Jeep magazines stacked on the coffee table.

"I can read some fascinating articles on how to install fender flares or third-row seats to you. Or you can choose from my selection of military fiction." He gestured to the built-in bookshelves on either side of the fireplace, where a dozen or so spines boasted titles promising intrigue and action.

During their high school years, he'd taken to reading to her from whatever book their English teacher had assigned. While the task had been meant to help him focus, it had helped distract her from her problems.

Rubbing her thumb over the mug, she recognized it as the same kind her mother had bought at the base exchange. Barbara had placed it in the kitchen window as a reminder of Thomas James—an accomplished, well-respected Force Recon Marine but a lousy husband and inconsistent father.

"You don't have a copy of *Jane Eyre* laying around?"

His blue eyes gleaming, he shook his head. "Afraid not."

"No *Great Expectations*?"

"If not for you, I wouldn't have *any* books in the house."

She experienced a pinprick of satisfaction. Knowing she'd played a small part in helping him become a reader—no matter what his choice of material—put a smile on her face.

Tori saw Cade's gaze shift to her mouth. Had it been that long since she'd smiled? Around him, probably. Awareness flared deep inside like a match in an underground cave. Shared memories thickened the air between them. Tori missed the security of his embrace, the thrill of his kiss. She missed their friendship. They'd had the kind of bond she'd thought was indestructible.

For two people with separate strengths—the popular jock and the shy bookworm—they'd built a mutually beneficial friendship. She'd helped him with his schoolwork. He'd pushed her socially, urging her to attend dances and football games when she'd preferred to stay home, curled up in her reading nook. They'd been each other's sounding boards. He'd vented about the family fishing business and his dad's expectations. She'd poured out her frustrations—her parents' fractious relationship, her father's inability to keep his promises, the annoyances that came with having a toddler brother. He'd listened and commiserated, never judging. Cade had always told her the truth, whether she'd liked it or not.

In the decade since she'd been gone, she'd hoped and wished and prayed for another relationship like theirs. No one had come close. Certainly not Patrick.

Thoughts of that spectacular failure chased away her smile.

Cade folded his arms over his chest and watched as she sipped her tea. While she'd been taking a shower in his guest bathroom, he'd changed into a pair of jeans and a black, long-sleeved cotton shirt emblazoned with the letters *USMC*. He looked tired but strong, capable of addressing any threat that landed on their doorstep.

He noticed her reassessing the windows overlooking

the front yard and the pair of French doors leading to the patio.

"The alarm system is activated."

"I know." She'd watched him do it.

Still, she felt unprepared. She didn't own a gun. Didn't know martial arts. She'd taken a self-defense class during her second year at university, but that had been years ago. Until now, she'd been living in a bubble, believing she'd be safe as long as she avoided the wrong areas of town and kept her wits about her.

She explored the fresh wrap on her wrist, which throbbed in time with her heartbeat. Fighting with Brandon had exacerbated the sprain. Her midsection was sore—probably from being carried like a sack of potatoes.

Her lungs seized anew with remembered panic.

Cade leaned in and covered her hand with his. His skin was hot to the touch, smooth in places and rough in others.

"We're going to catch him. We have plenty of clues. We just have to give the authorities time to do their jobs."

Tempted to cling to his hand, she disengaged and placed the mug on the table.

Linking his hands between his knees, he studied her from beneath hooded lids. "Tell me about Patrick."

"We're not discussing my romantic past. And I have no interest in hearing about yours, either."

Over the years, her mother had informed her of every woman who'd cast her net for Cade and cheerfully reported every time he rebuffed their advances. He'd claimed he wasn't interested in marriage. Barbara's theory? He'd never gotten over Tori.

She didn't buy it.

"This isn't personal," he said. "Maybe there's a connection between him and your current trouble."

"Because he's a convicted criminal?"

"He's proven he's not above breaking the law."

"Patrick's not your basic street thug. He's intelligent and ambitious."

Cade snorted.

"Patrick was the last person I'd suspect of any sort of crime, let alone embezzlement." She threw her hands up. "He had everything going for him. A solid career. Friends and family."

"And you." His face was completely devoid of emotion, blocking her from his thoughts. Surely this discussion was as strange for him as it was her. "How serious was it?"

"We had common interests." Thinking back, she realized they'd spent a majority of their time together in the company of friends. Had that been his preference? Or perhaps an unconscious decision of hers? Either way, he hadn't complained.

"Did you love him?"

Love him? She was beginning to suspect she wasn't capable of loving any man but Cade. "That has nothing to do with this situation."

He lifted his hands. "You're right. None of my business."

A thud outside the windows had Cade off the couch and reaching for his gun, a larger, meaner weapon than he'd had at the diner.

"You expecting someone?" she asked, her pulse skittering.

"Negative. Stay here."

When he was out of sight, Tori got up and crept after

him. The main entryway was around the corner from the living room.

His huff of surprise echoed to her. "It's your mom."

"What?"

A succession of beeps deactivated the alarm. Then he was welcoming Barbara James into his home.

Tori rushed to Cade's side. Barbara handed him a large container. "Mom, you shouldn't be here. Remember what I said at the hospital? I'm a danger magnet right now."

"What mother is going to stay away from her child when she's in need?" she chided. "I brought your favorite soup." She patted Cade's hand. "No chicken noodle for my girl. Italian wedding soup is the trick to making Tori feel better."

"That was thoughtful of you," he said and smiled for her benefit. He then did a quick scan of the street before closing the door and rearming the system.

The sight of her mom's fingers evoked a wave of emotion inside Tori. The knuckles were swollen and the area around her nails puffy and purple. She hated what the disease was doing to her beautiful, loving mother. But she admired Barbara's internal strength and unshakeable faith.

Tori hugged her. "You're always putting others' needs above your own."

"A trait passed on from mother to daughter," Cade said, admiration deepening his eyes to navy.

Pleasure warmed her. It had been a long time since Cade had looked at her like that.

In the kitchen, Cade poured coffee for Barbara and himself, while Tori nursed her tea.

"Your color's better." Seated on a stool at the center island, she patted the one beside her. Tori took the hint and sat.

"I feel almost normal," she reassured her. "Your soup will restore me to one hundred percent."

"The soup isn't the real reason I wanted to see you. I came to tell you I'm canceling my birthday party."

Tori shot off the seat. "Mom, more than a hundred guests have been invited. The venue's booked. The catering paid for. Flowers. Music. You can't cancel with less than twenty-four-hours' notice."

"I'm not celebrating my sixtieth without my daughter in attendance."

Tori settled her hands atop Barbara's shoulders. "Oh, Mom, you know I hate to miss it, but I don't think it's wise. Jason's promised to take tons of photos and videos. And Cade's mom is going to save us some cake."

Barbara jutted her chin, and the battle light in her eyes meant she wouldn't back down. "It's inconvenient, I know. And you and Dee have been busy planning for weeks. But we have to postpone. I've discussed it with her, and she agrees. We're going to make the calls tonight."

Tori sent Cade a help-me-talk-sense-into-her look.

There was a pensive set to his jaw. "The party's at the Topsail Inn, right? In a meeting space with a limited number of access points."

"What are you thinking?"

He held up his cell. "Let me make a few calls."

They waited in silence while he paced from fridge to stove and back. Ten minutes later, he flashed a tight smile. "I've lined up a few guys who've agreed to stand guard. Also, Deputy Clark does private security engagements on the side for a fee."

Barbara's face lit up. "Does this mean Tori can attend?"

"For an hour or two. And she stays at my side at all times."

"You're sure it's safe?" Barbara's excitement waned. "I don't mind canceling, honestly."

"I don't want to put anyone in danger," Tori said.

"The sketch of Brandon is being circulated on social media. My guess is he'll go into hiding for a while. Two of my buddies are Special Forces, three are Infantry, like me, and one's a pilot and martial arts instructor on the side."

Tori slowly nodded. "With the deputy there, too, he won't dare try anything."

Barbara rushed to hug Cade. "Thank you. You've always been like a son to me."

Over the top of Barbara's head, Cade sent Tori an indecipherable look. Was he wondering if he'd made the right call? Or, like her, was he thinking he'd be an official part of the family if things had turned out differently?

Whatever the case, she couldn't put into words how much she appreciated what he was doing for her and her mom. He was going above and beyond the call of duty, putting his safety on the line to ensure hers. Cade may have changed over the years, but he was still a hero at heart.

Sunday night, the party was in full swing when Cade ushered Tori inside the seaside inn as though she was a high-profile actress avoiding paparazzi. She didn't have time to enjoy the ocean view or twinkly white lights in the arched canopy above the entrance. Inside the quaint lobby, he steered her down a wooden-paneled hallway on their left.

"What did you do, study the inn's floor plans?"

"I asked a friend to scope out the venue." As they

drew closer to the meeting room, a stranger straightened from the wall opposite and stood like a sentinel, watching their approach.

Tori's stride faltered. Well over six feet and built like a tank, he could've been a magazine model or a member of the criminal underworld. Like Cade, he wore a tailored dark suit that fell somewhere between black and navy, an expertly knotted tie and immaculate dress shoes.

Cade's fingers tightened a fraction on her arm. "It's all right. Julian's part of your protection team."

His black hair was cut short, as per military standards, but the close-cut beard threw her off. "He's a civilian?"

"He's Force Recon."

"Like my father."

"Yes."

Cade greeted him with a hearty handshake. The man's gaze settled on her, curious and assessing. There was a world of mystery behind those brown eyes.

"Tori, I'd like you to meet a friend of mine, Julian Tan."

"Thank you for agreeing to come."

"I'm happy to help. Besides, you got me out of a shopping trip with my sister. For that, I'm grateful." His smile softened the angles of his face, which made him seem slightly less dangerous.

"Julian and I attend the same church. We've played on several basketball leagues together."

Julian clapped Cade on the back. "I tried to convince him to join us over at Force Recon, to no avail."

"Why didn't you?"

"I'm happy where I'm at." He shrugged.

"A shame," Julian said.

"Are the other guys in place?"

"Deputy Clark is patrolling the parking lot. The emergency exit is covered, as are the kitchen areas and rest-rooms. Your guy Johnson hasn't showed."

Cade's forehead bunched. "That's not like Brett."

He sent off a text message before guiding Tori inside the room that had been transformed from a basic meeting space to an elegant oasis. She felt guilty for not being able to help Cade's mom with last-minute preparations, but he had ruled it out of the question. Guests mingled while taking advantage of the hot buffet. She spotted her mom right away, chatting and laughing with her friends. The carefree delight on her face muted Tori's disquiet.

Her mom deserved to have a memorable birthday.

"Who's Johnson?"

Cade perused the room, his gaze going to the bank of windows overlooking the pier slicing into the Atlantic. "Staff Sergeant Brett Johnson. We met in boot camp." He checked his phone and frowned. "We haven't always been assigned to the same units, but we've kept in touch. We started working together again about eighteen months ago. He was supposed to help out tonight."

"Maybe he changed his mind."

"Maybe."

Chilled air from an overhead vent washed over her, raising goose bumps on her skin. Cade noticed her subtle shiver and deftly removed his suit jacket. Moving close, he draped it over her shoulders.

"Better?"

Tori nodded, the material's warmth cocooning her. She lifted her hands to hold the lapels together, and her fingers tangled with his. Their gazes caught and held. His mouth curved in an enigmatic smile before he lowered his hands to his sides.

Tori reminded herself that they weren't a couple out on a date. They weren't even together by choice. They'd been thrust into this storm and had no other option but to ride it out together.

"Let's go say hello to our mothers," he said, choosing to ignore the charged moment.

They were weaving through the sea of round tables when he received a call. His brows descending, he showed her the screen. "It's Claxton."

Tori listened to the brief, one-sided conversation. Cade's features hardened.

"They got a tip," he told her. "Brandon's real name is Aaron Waters. Former Marine Corps sergeant. He enlisted as an infantryman, but was pulled to Special Forces five years ago. Eighteen months ago, he sustained a shoulder injury that took three surgeries to correct. Marine Corps let him go via medical discharge in January, and he wasn't at all happy about it."

"We're dealing with a disgruntled, highly skilled Marine," she said. The photo Claxton texted to Cade showed a younger version of her attacker.

"Knowing his identity is a step in the right direction. They'll dig into his past. Find out who his friends are and maybe where he's been living since he was discharged."

Tearing her gaze away from the image, she said, "I still don't understand what he wants with me. If he wanted to kill me, he had the chance to do it in my apartment."

"It's possible he's part of a human trafficking ring. Maybe he lives in your area and became fixated on you. What other businesses do you frequent besides the bank?"

"I've been to the seafood market once or twice. The park a handful of times. I haven't spent too much time exploring."

"And you don't remember him? He hasn't come into The Canine Companion?"

"Not that I recall."

He motioned over his shoulder. "I'm going to show this photo to the guys on duty."

"I'll be with my mom."

Tori was glad for the break in the case. However, frustration needled her. Why would a random stranger target her?

After her mom introduced her to some friends she hadn't yet met, she pulled her behind the gift table. "How are you, darling?"

"My mind is clear, and I feel energized." The effects of the drug had worn off quickly.

"I didn't mean your physical state. How are you coping? On top of what happened at the apartment, it can't be easy spending every waking moment with Cade."

Without prompting, her gaze sought him out. His constant state of alertness showed in the way he carried himself, his body bristling with suppressed energy. He kept his right hand free, periodically brushing against his sidearm as if to reassure himself it was still there. Tori could almost picture him in enemy territory, a warrior decked in camo, willing and able to do whatever necessary to secure victory.

His body was honed into a human weapon. He was mentally tough, too. Any man who survived the rigorous boot camp at Parris Island had to be. Add to that years of training in harsh conditions—designed to prepare Marines for the realities of war—and she couldn't have asked for a better protector.

"Be honest, Mom. You'd like nothing more than to see us back together."

"I happen to think you're perfect for each other. You simply weren't ready at eighteen." At Tori's instant protest, she held up a finger. "However, I haven't been praying selfish prayers. I've asked the Lord to bring His chosen man into your life."

"You mean a civilian who doesn't embezzle money from his company?"

"You've always believed the best of people. Don't let your experience with Patrick make you cynical." Barbara patted her hand. "And I know your father's and my struggles tarnished your view of military life. There are things you don't know, Tori. Things I should've told you a long time ago."

"What things?"

The shriek of an alarm drowned out the musicians. The high-pitched pulse vibrated through the room, assaulting Tori's ears. Around them, some people froze, while others started calmly moving toward the exits.

"I don't smell smoke. Do you?" Barbara looked toward the kitchens.

"Not at all."

Tori searched the spacious room for Cade. When she didn't see him, her blood turned cold.

Was there a true emergency inside the inn or was her attacker here, waiting to pounce?

EIGHT

The alarm startled Cade. Outside in the hall, he spun toward the meeting room. "Tori."

Julian pulled his weapon from the shoulder holster hidden beneath his suit jacket. "Scattering everyone and luring them out into the open? Perfect opportunity to snatch her."

Together, they rushed inside. The space was rapidly emptying through a pair of exits no longer manned by his guys.

His stomach roiled. "I don't see her."

A few employees loitered near the buffet tables, unfazed by the continuing pulse of sound. "Is there a fire somewhere in the building?"

"The manager isn't sure what triggered the alarm. He's investigating now."

Cade and Julian threaded their way through the throng and exited into the muggy evening. He craned his neck for a better view.

"There."

Julian pointed to the corner of the building, where Jason, Heath Polanski and their dates formed a tight circle around Tori. Barbara and his mom stood close by, deep in conversation. His buddies, Fleming and Powers, flanked the group, alert and ready to defend.

"Anything strike you as unusual?" He scanned the utility buildings and employee parking lot. Sand dunes blocked the view of the beach.

"No, but this guy's proven his marksmanship skills. Let's get her back inside ASAP."

At their approach, Tori snagged his gaze and wouldn't let go. If this was an ordinary celebration, if her life wasn't in danger, he'd have trouble keeping his admiration in check. She'd surprised him by foregoing her usual demure skirts for a pair of slim, ankle-length black pants, chunky black sandals and a swingy, white sequined tank top that showcased her smooth shoulders and toned arms. She was stunning.

Hardly appropriate, McMann. Focus.

Heath turned to him. "Any clue what's going on, Staff Sergeant?"

"Not yet."

"You're off duty, dude." Jason nudged his friend. "No need to be formal."

"It's a sign of respect." Heath smirked and shook his head. "You'll understand one of these days. When are you taking the ASVAB?"

"Next week. I'm studying every chance I get. Cade's been giving me pointers, too."

Tori quickly squelched her look of surprise. Cade had agreed to help Jason study for the military entrance exams long before she'd returned. He didn't like going against her wishes, but he truly believed her brother would succeed in the Corps.

His date shot him an encouraging smile. "You're gonna ace it, Jason. Before you know it, you'll be wearing the uniform."

"Thanks, Jill."

Cade made his way to Tori's side, his fingers skimming her wrist. "Okay?"

"Fine." The breeze teased her hair, pushing it into her eyes. Without thinking, Cade moved to dislodge it, threading the pearlescent strands behind her ear. Shimmery lip gloss emphasized the shape of her lips.

He banished that thought. Kissing her was out of the question.

"Did you know my sister is against me enlisting?"

Tori's breath caught. Her cheeks pinked. "Jason, we should discuss this later."

His eyes challenged her. "I simply find it ironic that you're eager to accept the protection of these Marines." He gestured to Julian and the others. "But you don't want me to serve, and you don't want anything to do with anyone who does."

"Tori's right," Cade intervened. "This is hardly the time."

While he understood Jason's frustration, this wasn't the time or place for this discussion.

Jill, along with Heath's date, slipped away, affording the siblings privacy. Heath lingered. Annoyed, Cade flashed a look at the lance corporal that he correctly interpreted and went to join the women.

"I respect and admire our military men and women and their families," Tori said. "I appreciate their sacrifices."

The image of her father's flag-draped casket pulsed through his mind, the sharp, body-jolting reports of the guns' salute an echo of loss and grief. Thomas died twelve years ago. Tori had been sixteen and Jason only six. Her experiences involving her father were vastly different from Jason's.

The quick flare of anger was snuffed out in Jason's

face, but resentment smoldered. Cade didn't think Tori was aware just how much her choice to live elsewhere had hurt the boy.

"You can't keep me in a cocoon. There are risks to any job. I could get hurt at the factory. One year ago, a guy died because a forklift fell on him. There are accidents on Cade's dad's fishing boats." He tugged on the knot in his tie. "At least I'll have proper training in the Corps."

A fire truck lumbered down the side road and rounded the building, out of sight. Julian and the others stood stoically a few yards away, watching the crowd.

"You're too young to remember the bad times." Sadness tinged her tone. "The demands of the military destroyed our parents' marriage."

"Who said I was going into Special Forces? Who's to say I'm anything like Dad?"

"What happens when you meet someone and fall in love?" She gestured to Jill. "Guaranteed you'll get relocated to Japan or California. She may not be willing to move with you and leave her family and career behind."

"I may be a kid in your eyes, sis, but from what I've seen, love involves sacrifice. If two people truly love each other, they'll do anything to be together."

He flicked a significant glance at Cade, his meaning abundantly clear—she hadn't loved Cade enough to make it work.

"Jason, cut your sister some slack. She cares about you—"

"How can you defend her?" he burst out, his eyes stormy. "She abandoned you just like she abandoned me."

Tori reeled back, flinching as if he'd plunged a knife deep into her chest and twisted.

"She didn't cut you out of her life. She visited you. Sent letters. Birthday presents."

Rolling his eyes, he muttered, "Forget it."

Jason rejoined his friends and the group meandered closer to the dunes.

Tori sagged against the brick facade, defeat a cloak around her.

"Give him time."

"We won't have a lot of that if he enlists." She twisted her silver ring. "He'll be in boot camp for three months, then infantry school. Who knows where he'll be stationed. One of the benefits of coming home was to make up for lost time."

"I understand. And deep down, he does, too. But you can't expect him to change his plans now that you've suddenly decided to return home. He has the right to carve his own path, the same as you did."

"I feel like the tentative thread holding us together is unraveling," she murmured. "You could encourage him to go to college."

Cade shook his head. "He doesn't want that. At least not now. He's more like me than you in the academic realm."

"You've experienced the reality of war. Have you prepared him for that? Or did you gloss over the gritty details and paint the hero-in-dress-blues poster, the same spiel every recruiter doles out?" Her lips trembled. "He's my only sibling, Cade. Would you have me lose him, too?"

"No one knows what I went through over there besides my brothers," he said, using the term for other Marines. "So no, I didn't give him a play-by-play. Nor did I pull the wool over his eyes. Like you, he's acquainted with the price that serving our country sometimes demands."

"You refuse to dissuade him, then?"

"I couldn't even if I tried."

"I see."

He exhaled. "Tori—"

"False alarm, folks." The inn manager waved everyone inside. "You're free to return to the festivities."

Julian discreetly re-holstered his weapon. "What's the plan, McMann? Stay or leave?"

Cade scrutinized their surroundings. "This could've been our guy creating a diversion. Have Deputy Clark do a thorough check of my vehicle while I take Tori inside. We'll leave when I'm satisfied he's not in the area."

"Done."

Inside the meeting space, Cade remained by her side, as promised. Tori didn't say much, but her eyes told of her turmoil. He wished Jason had waited to vent his frustration, but the kid was eighteen and impulsive. He had maturing to do. The drill instructors at boot camp would take care of that.

Still, Tori didn't need the added pressure. She had enough to deal with.

"You hungry?"

"Not really. I guess I should sample the food your mom and I ordered, though."

At the buffet tables, Cade was handing her a plate when his parents descended.

"Don't you look lovely tonight." Dee enfolded Tori in a maternal embrace. Always a fan of his best-friend-turned-sweetheart, she had been outspoken about her hopes they'd reconcile someday. "What do you think of the decorations?"

Tori glanced around the space with an appreciative eye. "Your suggestion of a silver-and-white theme was a good one. The bouquets are gorgeous."

Each silver-draped table was graced with a different assortment of white blossoms—peonies, hydrangeas and roses—in simple glass vases. Gardenias perfumed the air with a light, pleasant scent.

"Do you think your mom is pleased?"

"Most definitely. She's fortunate to have you as her best friend." Tori's shoulders drooped. "I'm sorry I wasn't able to help with last-minute preparations."

Dee gestured to Cade's dad, who, as usual, let his wife carry the conversation. Paul McMann was at home on the open water. Parties weren't high on his list of what counted as entertainment. He was only here out of respect for their longtime friend.

"Paul and I are praying they catch this guy soon," Dee said. "I'm glad Cade is able to be with you."

Tori's gaze roved over his suit, lingering on the arm that got clipped. "I wish he hadn't gotten injured on account of me. I did try to talk him out of volunteering to be my bodyguard. You can guess how that went."

Dee's eyes shined with pride and she gave him a side hug. "He's a tough cookie. And he knows how to handle himself in dangerous situations, thanks to his training. Isn't that right, Paul?"

His dad's lips pursed. "My son has a mind of his own. If he'd determined to protect you, Tori, you wouldn't be able to dissuade him."

With that, he marched to the drink station and ordered a root beer.

A pained expression marred his mother's youthful face. She was the only one in his family who hadn't condemned his decision to walk away from the family business. Being a Marine wasn't the problem. His dad, uncle and cousins would've been just as upset if he'd chosen to be a pastor or a police officer. He'd bucked tradition, turned his back on the family legacy, and they'd never fully forgiven him for it.

Paul had taken it the hardest. Since Cade's birth, he'd planned to hand McMann Family Fishing over to his only son. Cade hadn't minded the work. He liked being on the water, liked seeing the fruits of hard labor and teamwork. But fishing wasn't in his blood. Wasn't his passion. Defending his country, working alongside men whom he considered his brothers, was his calling. As with Tori, he'd bundled things. He should've prepared his father instead of showing up with the signed enlistment papers in hand. What a spectacular lack of judgment. Paul had been furious. Hurt, too, but he'd buried that. To this day, he refused to discuss the subject. He hadn't once told Cade he was proud of him. It was an old hurt that flared up occasionally, one that Cade had prayed over many times.

"Never mind him," Dee tried to gloss over the awkward moment. "He's grumpy because I forced him to wear a suit and tie."

"No need to make excuses for him, Mom," Cade told her, keeping his voice even. "Let's eat. I have to get Cinderella home long before midnight."

After filling their plates, they ate at a table situated close to the musicians. Cade couldn't relax and enjoy the meal. His attention bounced among the various exits, as well as the kitchen area where the employees came and went. They wore matching uniforms, which consisted of black pants, white shirts and black vests. It would be easy for Aaron Waters to blend in. As a member of Special Forces, he would've been taught the art of subterfuge.

Tori leaned close, her shoulder pressing into his. "You don't think he'd plant another bomb, do you? Is that what you sent Clark to look for?"

Hearing the tremor in her voice, the disquiet she tried valiantly to mask, he found her hand beneath the table and squeezed it. "I was thinking more of a tracking device. Don't worry. If I know Julian, he'll do an inspection of his own."

The words had no sooner left his mouth when Julian entered the room and gave him a thumbs-up.

"We're good to leave." Anxious to get her home, he glanced at her half-empty plate. "We should probably head out soon."

After placing her napkin over the uneaten portion, she gathered her clutch purse and scooted her chair back. "I'm ready. Let's tell our mothers goodbye."

As he and Tori took turns hugging Dee and Barbara and expressing their regrets, Cade caught them exchanging significant looks. He sensed their renewed hope. Foolhardy hope. Tori's reasons for refusing to marry him hadn't changed. He was and always would be a Marine. His career was an insurmountable obstacle between them.

Wishing she'd accept his choice, support his dreams and aspirations, like he would do for her, was a waste of time. He'd accepted that a long time ago.

It was a relief to head home. Only when they were tucked in his house, the alarm activated, would he be able to relax.

Tori took her spot in the passenger seat, her fingers not immediately releasing the door handle. "Do you think he's out there, watching us?"

"My guys did a thorough sweep of the inn and the neighboring businesses. There's no reason to think Aaron was involved." When her brow remained knitted with worry, he tacked on, "A kid could've pulled the alarm."

A sigh whistling through her pursed lips, she let her head sink against the headrest. "I'm glad Mom didn't cancel her party, but that was intense. And an inconvenience for your friends. I have to make Angela understand why my presence at her party isn't worth it." She paused. "I'll make it up to her somehow. She has a weakness for expensive perfume."

"Your life will go back to normal, Tori. Don't lose sight of that."

"I'm trying." She attempted a smile, but it was a weak imitation of the real thing. "I'm sorry about earlier. I was wrong to take my frustration about Jason out on you."

Dusk had descended, painting the ocean and distant sky in a pinkish-yellow haze. The parking lot lights had flickered on. Lowering his gaze, he saw the faint outline of blue veins on the inside of her wrist. She had the prettiest skin…like moonlight bathing a frozen winter lake in pearlescent light. He was tempted to hold her hand. Bring it to his lips and brush a kiss there.

He loosened his tie and, pulling it over his head, laid it on the back seat, atop his discarded suit jacket. He eased his top shirt button free and rolled his sleeves up. Starting the Jeep's engine, he forced his mind on practical matters and started for the lot exit. Julian was behind them in his sleek black Corvette and would follow them home.

"I don't like being at odds with you. I miss our friendship. We used to make each other laugh, remember?"

Her breath hitched. "I remember."

They left the stretch of beach and small motels behind and crossed a high, dark bridge.

"I meant what I said back there. I'm grateful for what you do, for all the men and women who defend our country."

Cade's heart pounded heavily in his chest. Her admission didn't alter their relationship, but it did soothe old wounds.

"I simply couldn't live that life again, not after my dad…" She huffed out a dry laugh. "I used to daydream that he had a regular job."

"You wished he was a baker."

"That's right. Then I could've had as many pastries as I wanted."

"You also mentioned a traveling-circus owner."

"I forgot about that one. I would've liked to try my hand at the high ropes. Jason would've wanted to do the motorcycle stunts." Shaking her head, she said, "It's wrong, I know, but I used to wish he wasn't a hero."

He didn't blame her for feeling that way. She'd been a young girl longing for her father's love and guidance. Instead, she'd been served one disappointment after another.

He rested one hand on the wheel. "Knowing what I know now, he could've made things easier on the three of you. I've met Special Forces guys who have families. Not only do they make it work, they're happy."

A shadow passed over her face. "You think he liked the secrecy?"

"I'm saying he might've taken on more than he had to."

"To get away from my mom?"

"Maybe it was easier to focus on his job than deal with problems at home."

Tori mulled over Cade's words. Just before the fire alarm, her mom had suggested there were things about their marriage she didn't know. But what?

Cade's phone buzzed. After a brief exchange, he ended the call. "Julian's got to run by Courthouse Bay. Something about preparations for an upcoming mission."

In the side mirror, she saw his Corvette turn off.

"We're not far from your place."

"Ten minutes."

Headlights from an approaching car temporarily blinded her. Instead of taking the highway, Cade had chosen an indirect route of secondary roads. This particular one ran alongside government land. There were no neighborhoods or gas stations, so they'd encountered only a handful of vehicles. Dusk had given way to complete night. Moonlight frosted the tips of the dense pines on either side.

In her side mirror, she saw what looked to be twin headlights, but they were too far apart to be a car.

"Are those motorcycles?"

Cade cracked his window. "Sounds like it."

The lights approached at amazing speed. "They're going fast."

"This is a good place to race without getting caught. Too often, junior Marines find themselves with cash on hand and no parents around to give input on their purchases. Bikes are cheaper than cars. Insurance is minimal." He gauged their approach with a deepening frown. "These guys are going to find themselves in jail or the ER if they don't slow down."

The roar of their engines got louder. Cade tapped the brake, clearly expecting them to pass him on this long stretch of straight pavement.

They didn't pass.

The rear window shattered and glass rained onto the back seat.

"Get down!" Cade shouted, jerking the Jeep into the oncoming lane and gunning the engine.

Tori hunkered in the seat, her gaze fixed on Cade. He divided his attention between the road ahead and the sport bikes in the mirror. She prayed like she'd never prayed before.

The Jeep couldn't outrun them. Their only hope was to outmaneuver them.

Aaron Waters had a partner.

Another bullet hit its mark, pinging off her side mirror. She screamed.

Cade grabbed her hand and guided it to the wheel. "Take it."

"What are you going to do?" she gasped, trying to stay low while also keeping the vehicle on the road.

"Convince them to leave."

He removed his gun and, twisting halfway around, got off two shots. But the Jeep was slowing. If those guys managed to pull alongside and shoot point-blank—

"Missed," he muttered.

Facing forward again, he resumed the wheel and their speed. Above the straining engines, Tori thought she heard a pop. Like the sound of a balloon bursting.

"They shot the tire!" he warned, straining with the wheel.

One minute they were racing down the deserted road, the next they were careening out of control. The Jeep tipped over and landed with a thundering jolt on Cade's side. Tori's seat belt dug into her torso, holding her fast against the seat. Metal crunched. Glass pricked her skin like a hundred tiny needles.

The trees rushed at them.

"Cade!"

Tori squeezed her eyes shut. *Please, God...*

The impact shuddered through the vehicle. It rocked several times and then heaved to a sudden stop, jarring her body. The whir of a spinning tire in midair became clear, as did the hiss of the Jeep's engine. Smoke curled out of the hood. Images of her car going up in flames spurred her to fumble for her seat belt.

"We have to get out."

Cade didn't answer. Tori looked over, her neck protesting the movement, and saw blood trickling down his temple. His eyes were closed, his head at an awkward angle, his hands limp.

Fear and denial forged into full-blown terror. "Cade! Wake up!"

She tried to reach him, but he was slumped against the door, which was wedged against a sapling tree.

"Talk to me."

Tori managed to release the clasp. She tumbled against him.

Trying to find a spot to support her weight, she pressed her hand to his cheek. "I need you to wake up."

In the distance, she heard the motorcycles. They were turning around. Coming to ensure they'd finished the job. Adrenaline spiked.

If they didn't get out of this Jeep in the next few minutes, escape would be impossible.

NINE

Fingers whispered over Cade's face, luring him from the brink of unconsciousness. He focused on the gentle touch to try to block the intense pain in his head.

Someone gave his shoulder a rough shake.

"Cade, open your eyes." The voice was insistent. "We're in trouble."

For a second, he was back in the sand pit, IEDs exploding. Gunfire threatening his men.

"They're coming back. We have to get out!"

"Tori?" His lids were heavy, his body sluggish.

"Thank the Lord, you're awake." She sighed, cradling his cheek. "Are you able to move? Is anything broken?"

"Head's about to explode. That's the worst of it." Blinking to clear his vision, he did a quick survey of her. He couldn't see much in the dark. The Jeep rested at an odd angle, and she was working to stay upright and not topple onto him. "What about you?"

"Fine." Balancing against the seat, she fumbled for something beneath his legs. "Found your gun." She released his seat belt and squeezed his shoulder. "Take my hand. I'm gonna guide you out."

She clambered out of her door and then reached back for him. Movement exacerbated the pain, but his neck didn't protest and there wasn't any numbness in his extremities. The rollfover hadn't injured his spine. Or impaired his hearing.

Their assailants were getting closer, and his and Tori's window of escape was narrowing.

He had thirteen bullets left and no idea how much firepower their enemies had.

Cade crawled out of his seat. Fighting nausea, he used the dashboard and seat to work his way to the top. Tori grabbed his hand and assisted him onto solid ground.

Twin lights bore down on them.

"Wait. My phone."

"I have mine." She patted her pocket. "Let's go." Threading her fingers through his, she motioned with his gun, urging him toward the woods.

He clung to her hand, grateful for the cover of darkness and praising God their injuries were minor. Tori's calm astounded him. His already high admiration inched up another notch.

Several hundred yards in, he slowed.

She turned, her hair gleaming in the vague light. "What's wrong?"

"This may be our best chance to find out who's working with Aaron."

"You want to go back?"

"I want this to end," he ground out. "Can I see your phone?"

She complied. The screen lit up, showing zero service. "No signal." He surveyed their surroundings. "I've trained in these woods. Not far from here is a dirt road that will take you to the main highway. There you can flag a passing vehicle."

"No. We are not splitting up."

"Tori, we've been fortunate so far—"

"God's got us in the palm of His hand. We'll get answers. Just not like this." She started backing up. "We'll go to the facility together." Her tone brooked no argument.

Behind him, the noise crested and then cut off abruptly. They would soon learn he and Tori hadn't died in the wreck and would hunt for them. If he had more time, if his body wasn't threatening mutiny between the dizziness and queasy stomach, he'd attempt to reason with her.

"I forgot how hardheaded you can be," he muttered, falling into step with her. Each jar of his foot against the earth sent arcs of lightning from his left temple to his ear.

"When the situation calls for it, I can be as stubborn as you."

Venturing deeper into the wooded terrain, their ragged breathing and the sweep of their shoes on the pine-needle bed below were too loud in the hushed night.

Tori seized his wrist. "Did you hear that? Sounded like a twig or branch snapping."

He scrutinized the way they'd come, shadows melding into an impenetrable mass. "Let's keep moving."

They walked as fast as they dared, given the limited light. He worried about holes that could twist or break an ankle. And snakes. There'd even been bear sightings through the years.

Cade had trained in this general area multiple times during his career, both as a green Marine and at a more advanced rank. The weather hadn't always been kind and the difficulties had varied. He'd been wet and cold. He'd been hot to the point of heat exhaustion. There'd been times he'd gotten lost. Times he'd gone hungry.

None of that had incited the level of fear and uncertainty he was currently battling. This time, the threat was real. There were no navy corpsmen waiting in the wings to patch up broken bones or administer fluids, no commanding officers to call a halt to the exercise.

Tori's well-being weighed heavily on him.

The shot, when it came, splintered the tree by his head. Bark flew in all directions.

Tori ducked. Cade pushed her behind another tree and ordered her to the ground.

He crouched, waiting and watching for his target to show.

There. A glint of moonlight on a visor.

Cade took aim and pulled the trigger.

A grunt of surprise, followed by a growled oath, was his reward. Time to run.

Without a word, he took hold of Tori's arm and helped her to stand. They jogged through the woods as fast as they dared. Once they reached the dirt track, they could increase their speed. If they made it before the others caught up.

Tori trusted Cade to lead them in the right direction. They navigated the isolated terrain, struggling through underbrush and dodging spindly branches of dead trees that could poke out an eye. Her bare arms prickled from the scratches and scrapes she would see come morning— assuming they managed to evade the ruthless men hunting them.

Her heart strained against her ribs, spurred by frequent jolts of fear originating in her midsection. Tori sucked in the pine-scented air. She reminded herself that Cade's familiarity with these woods had to count for something. And the fact that one of them had been shot.

"Do you think they stuck around?"

Cade shouldered between a massive tree and thick bushes, allowing her to pass while he held the overgrowth at bay. "There's a fifty-fifty chance the wound wasn't enough to deter them. They could've split up."

"Eventually someone else will drive along and see your Jeep. They'll contact the police."

"How long that might be is anyone's guess."

The heel of her shoe snagged on an exposed tree root, and she pitched forward. Thanks to Cade's quick reflexes, she didn't land face-first in the dirt.

"If I'd known I was going for a moonlit hike, I would've been better prepared."

"You didn't twist your ankle, did you?"

"I'm good." Belatedly, she realized she had an iron-grip on Cade's upper arms. She released him and resumed walking.

Cade snagged her hand. "Hold on."

At the odd inflection in his voice, she froze. Woodland sounds pressed in. Crickets chirping. Small animals scurrying—or slithering—along the ground. The occasional frog's bellow.

Tori was about to speak when the rhythmic scuff of shoes against earth reached her on the still night air. Her stomach clenched.

Cade dropped to his knees and mutely pulled her down beside him. After jabbing a finger at the bushes they'd just walked past, he indicated she should follow him. Her panted breaths accosted her ears. Surely they could hear her frantic heartbeat, sense the terror pouring off her in waves.

Pulling up the lowest section, he waited for her to crawl into the hollow area inside. Dirt seeped beneath her fingernails. Knobby wood poked her neck and shoulders as she scooted over to make room for Cade. It was tight. His big body crowded her as he eased his weapon from its holster.

A tickle on her exposed neck made her imagine a black widow spider crawling on her like one she'd discovered on her deck chair. Fat black body with the bloodred warning on its abdomen. A shudder worked through her. When the creepy-crawly sensation coursed along her spine, she yelped.

Yards from their hiding spot, the steps ceased. "Did you hear something?"

Aaron's voice arrowed inside, freezing the blood in her veins.

Cade's arm came around her, a silent warning.

"Easy," he whispered.

The other man grunted in the negative. They stayed where they were for long, agonizing minutes. Cade's body heat leached into her, his soft cotton sleeves a comfort against her irritated skin.

"Let's keep moving," Aaron finally decreed.

When they'd gone, Cade removed his arm and said quietly, "I want you to stay here while I follow them."

Tori rejected that outright. "I don't think it's a good idea to split up. If you do have a concussion, you could become disoriented." Cade veering off course and becoming lost wasn't her only concern. The prospect of being left behind in these unfamiliar woods in the dead of night filled her with apprehension. "We should stay together."

She waited for him to launch a counterargument. Instead, he nodded. "Okay."

Cade exited and helped her to stand. At first, the pace was slow going and cautious, but soon became punishing. Her lungs were tight in her chest and her legs protesting when Cade pointed out a squat building up ahead. Its olive green exterior helped it blend with the trees. It had one window and a single locked door.

"We'll rest here a few minutes."

She knew good and well he didn't need rest. "I'm fine, Cade."

"You were in the hospital yesterday." He tested the window. Shut tight. He jiggled the knob. "Fortunately for us, no one's gotten around to updating the lock. It's a spring bolt." Tucking his gun in his holster, he took out his wallet and chose a store loyalty card.

"You know how to break in using a plastic card?"

"You'd be surprised at what I've learned during my time of service."

Tori positioned the phone so he could see, her ears attuned to any out-of-ordinary sounds. Was it too much to hope for that Aaron and his goon had given up the search?

He worked the card between the door and frame. He wiggled the card and, releasing the latch, pushed the door open.

"I can't believe you managed that."

They entered the musty building that smelled strongly of oil. The light glanced off containers of what was probably gasoline against the far wall.

"In my defense, I've never broken into anyone else's residence. Only my own. You wouldn't believe how many times I used to forget my keys inside my barracks room."

"There wasn't a master set somewhere?"

"Oh, I'm sure there was, but I didn't want the higher-ups to hear about my irresponsibility. So I took care of the problem myself."

She turned the light toward him. "You're bleeding pretty bad. Got a first-aid kit hidden in one of those pockets?"

He explored the skin around the gash on his temple. "I'm sure it looks much worse than it is."

"There's nothing in here of use, is there?"

His fingers closed over her wrist. "Don't worry about it."

"I am worried, Cade. We don't know how hard you hit your head."

"I distinctly remember the doctor ordering *you* to rest and avoid undue stress." His touch became a caress. "We'll both get an evaluation as soon as we make it out of these woods."

The near-darkness and isolation, combined with the high emotions accompanying the situation, threatened to topple Tori's defenses. She longed to seek solace in his arms. Instead, she found a relatively clean spot against the wall opposite the door and sank to the floor, wearier than she'd realized.

Cade headed for the door. "I'll be right outside."

"Wait, you're not staying in here?"

"We need a lookout."

She pushed to a standing position, hating that her legs felt like gelatin and hoping he didn't notice. "I'm not hiding in here, safe and protected, while you're in the open. I'll *rest* where you rest."

"Don't be stubborn—"

The door crashed open. A masked figure barreled into Cade. The men landed on the floor, each one jostling for position, a blur of thrusts and punches.

"Tori, run," Cade grunted.

Dashing out of the way, she searched the shelves for a weapon. A gasoline container would have to do. If she could strike the man hard enough to stun him, even for a minute, it would give Cade an edge.

The cocking of a gun had her spinning around. Moonlight bathed the second man in scant light. Aaron stalked toward her, a satisfied gleam in his eyes.

"Hello, Tori."

Dread curdled her stomach. She inched backward until the shelves dug into her shoulder blades.

Cade dodged his attacker and leaped to his feet, short of breath and fresh blood oozing from his head wound. "Don't you dare touch her."

The masked man also gained his feet and produced a gun, which he trained on Cade. He was shorter and slighter, but he'd obviously been trained in hand-to-hand combat. And there was no evidence he'd been injured, which meant Aaron was the one who'd been hit.

Aaron's weapon pointed at her head, he kept coming. He was walking fine. But he held the gun at an awkward angle, like he wasn't used to holding it with that hand. She couldn't see bloodstains on his black hoodie. Too dark.

She could see his twisted smile, however. It struck terror in her heart. They were trapped. Vulnerable to this madman's whims.

"Why are you doing this?" she demanded, her nails digging into her palms.

His hand clamped on to her nape, and he yanked her closer. Cigarette smoke clung to him.

He ran the tip of the gun barrel past her temple and along her cheek before jamming it beneath her chin. A whimper escaped.

Cade lunged.

Aaron reacted with lightning-fast reflexes, maneuvering her in front of him. His arm clamped on to her waist. She was under his control again. Only this time, she didn't have drugs making everything fuzzy and dream-like.

"Give my friend here your weapon," he ordered.

Cade's reluctance plain, he removed it from his holster

and dropped it to the ground. The masked man kicked it beneath the shelves.

"You're postponing the inevitable, Cade," he taunted. "You will pay for what you did. You and your girlfriend. But she's first. You'll see what it's like to suffer."

Tori's heart squeezed into a tight ball. This was about Cade?

"What are you talking about?" His voice shook with fury. "What did I do, Aaron?"

"Two words. William Poole."

The name sounded familiar. Tori racked her brain. Then it hit her. The Marine who'd died during Cade's last deployment. Aaron must blame him for William's death.

"William was a good man. You were close to him?" Cade asked.

"Like brothers," Aaron growled.

Aaron shifted, and the distinct coppery odor of blood hit her. She angled her face and caught sight of the slippery substance on his upper arm.

"You weren't stationed with us," Cade said. "You didn't see what happened during the foot patrol. We were ambushed."

"You were in charge. You ignored orders to return to the FOB."

FOB? What did that stand for?

Then she remembered. Forward Operating Base.

"That's not how it went down. You're acting on false information." Cade shook his head, frustration evident in his strained features. "Let Tori go, and I'll walk you through everything that happened that day."

Aaron snickered. The cold metal dug into her skin. What was his plan? Shoot her in front of Cade as some sort of sick revenge?

He started to propel her toward the door. "The next time you see her, she'll be in pieces."

Cade audibly inhaled.

Tori couldn't overpower or outfight her captor. But she could create an opening for Cade.

Sending up a desperate prayer, she reached up and dug her fingers into Aaron's wound.

He howled in her ear and lost his grip on her. Cade spun around, knocking the gun from the masked man's hand and sending it flying. He landed a kick in the man's midsection. The man hit the wall behind him and doubled over.

Tori slammed her heel into Aaron's boot. Spouting his fury, he tried to regain control over her. She struggled and thrashed.

And then Cade was there, his arm around Aaron's neck, cutting off his air supply.

The second man abandoned the fight and darted through the open door.

Tori managed to wrest free. She combed the cement floor for his abandoned gun.

"Found it," she called out.

Turning, she watched as Aaron slumped to the floor.

TEN

"Is he dead?" Tori demanded with a mixture of horror and relief.

"Unconscious." Cade grabbed the gun Aaron had dropped and tucked it into his waistband. "But not for long."

Charged on high emotion, Cade went and wrapped his arms around her. "You were so brave," he murmured against her hair. Tucked against his chest, she was warm and soft and *alive*.

Thank you, Lord, for Tori's quick thinking.

He'd tasted fear before. Sensed the scepter of death swinging for him more than once. This was worse. This was Tori's life on the line. He couldn't lose her. Having her in his life again—as a friend—was a priceless gift. He wasn't willing to give that up.

Dropping a kiss on her cheek, he nodded to the gun in her hand. "It's doubtful our second guy left prints. He had gloves on. But it might be registered to him."

"You think he's another friend of the fallen Marine?"

"Or he's being paid to help Aaron." He crossed to the doorway and studied the woods. "He bolted at the first opportunity. Doesn't speak of loyalty or conviction." He mentally wrestled with the bomb Aaron had detonated.

"We've been searching for someone in *your* life, *your* past, when in fact you're in danger because of me."

Her cool fingers encircled his forearm. "We'll figure this out."

"You've been home little more than a month, and until the car explosion, we hadn't spent time together."

"Aaron learned of our history somehow. Maybe he did some digging into your life. Talked to your friends or Marines you work with."

"The only one who knows about us is Brett."

"The one who didn't show at Mom's party?"

"He's not one to run his mouth. He wouldn't have told anyone."

When Cade had called and explained the situation with Tori, Brett had voiced his concern. He'd pointed out the potential problems that might arise from spending time with her. He'd even tried to convince Cade to leave her safety to someone else. As if that were possible.

Aaron groaned.

Tori swallowed hard. "What are we going to do with him?"

"With no phone signal, we're going to have to escort him back to the main road and flag someone down."

After retrieving his gun from beneath the shelves, he nudged Aaron with his boot. "Get up."

Aaron slowly came awake and gripped his head.

"Yeah, you're gonna have a bit of a headache." Cade wrestled with the urge to vent his loathing on the man who'd attacked Tori. "Let's go."

When he didn't budge, Cade aimed his Beretta at him. "Give me an excuse to shoot you," he dared. "You're familiar with the damage hollow-point bullets can do, I'm sure."

Grimacing, Aaron shuffled to his feet and preceded

them through the door. On the dirt track, he said, "If you think this ends with me, you're wrong."

The full moon hung high in the black sky, which was good. He was reluctant to use the phone's flashlight in case Aaron's buddy had hung around.

Walking close beside Cade, Tori sent him a worried glance.

"Oh, yeah?" he replied. "Your friend deserted you. What makes you think he's still interested in helping you?"

"He didn't desert me. He went for reinforcements."

The revelation that there were more who shared Aaron's skewed outlook troubled Cade. They needed to get to the main road as soon as possible. By now, someone must've come along and called the authorities.

He prodded Aaron's shoulder. "Pick up the pace."

"I've lost a lot of blood. Thanks to you, I've got a killer headache." He glanced behind him. "You got anything that can help me feel better, Tori?"

Cade's blood boiling, he seized the man's throat in a punishing grip. "You don't talk to her. You don't look at her. Understand?"

He chuckled. "You got it bad for the librarian, don't you?"

"How did you know about that?" Tori demanded.

"Oh, I know a lot of things, like how you dumped Mc-Mann and fled to Knoxville. I know you have a thing for bad boys."

Tori gripped Cade's arm. "He found out about Patrick."

"Who tipped you off about our past?" Cade asked. "Who's driving this plan? Because you don't strike me as capable of being the brains of an operation."

He clamped his mouth tight, finished talking for the moment.

Shoving him away, Cade nodded at the track. "Maybe you'll feel like answering the police's questions once you're wearing metal bracelets."

They walked in tense silence along the track. A half hour passed before they reached the point where he and Tori had exited the woods earlier.

"I'm dizzy and dehydrated," Aaron announced. "I need to sit."

"Negative. Keep going."

His accomplice had had ample time to regroup. It was anyone's guess whether he'd called for backup or fled the scene.

The woods were eerily quiet. No birds singing. No wind.

Cade divided his concentration between navigating them to the right spot and watching for unwelcome guests. He estimated they were halfway to the main road and had about another twenty minutes' walk. Tori remained quiet. She didn't complain, even though she had to be exhausted and scared.

In the distance, a motorcycle engine revved. Cade did a full circle, scanning the terrain. There were no lights to indicate it was nearby. Was the accomplice coming back to attempt a rescue?

Aaron stumbled and fell to his knees in the dirt. Cade moved to seize his arm, but Aaron vaulted up. The glint of a knife blade registered too late. Tori called out a warning just as searing pain sliced across his thigh.

Aaron's fist connected with Cade's cheek, inches from the gash on his temple. Dazed, he worked to stay upright. He couldn't prevent Aaron from knocking the gun from his grasp.

When he bolted in the direction of the motorcycle, Cade removed Aaron's own weapon from his waistband and got off two shots. The sound of his retreating steps meant he'd missed.

Tori rushed to his side and curved her arm around his waist, steadying him.

"How bad is it?"

"I'll live." He wasn't going to shine the light to inspect the wound. "We have to hurry, Tori. Can't let them circle back."

He wasn't functioning at 100 percent, and their enemies weren't above taking advantage. But then, Aaron also needed medical attention.

He threaded his fingers through hers and, ignoring the nagging sting in his leg, forged a path between the complicated network of pines. He could hear her whispered prayers and added his own silent entreaties. Without God's guidance and protection, they weren't going to survive long enough to discover the other players in this deadly game.

When flashing blue-and-red lights pierced the shadows, Tori squeezed his hand and picked up the pace. But as they approached the tree line, he dragged his feet.

"What's wrong?"

"Between us, we have three weapons, two of which aren't ours. They're going to have a lot of questions."

"We'll explain everything."

He gave a tight nod. Together, they entered the circles of light coming from the cruisers parked behind his wrecked Jeep. The sight of the mangled metal and splintered glass twisted his stomach into knots. They could've been gravely injured or even killed. God had protected them. Had been since the beginning.

A deputy spotted them. With a word to his partner, he

strode between the Jeep and the first cruiser. "You the owner of this Jeep?"

"Yes, sir. The name's Cade McMann. This is Tori James. We were run off the road and ambushed in the woods. The perpetrators are still at large. One of the men who's after us is Aaron Waters, retired Marine." He could see the other officer typing the information into his handheld device. "During the scuffle, we managed to get their weapons. Tori has one. Mine is in my holster and the other is here." Keeping the barrel pointed to the ground, he slowly held it out for them to see.

At this, the first officer pulled his gun and the second one strode over. "On your knees. Both of you."

"He's wounded," Tori protested. "Aaron had a knife."

"We'll take your statements once we've secured the weapons, ma'am."

"It's okay," Cade told her, complying with the order. "We've done nothing wrong."

The officers' stern demeanors didn't ease until their IDs had been run through the system and their story confirmed with Deputy Claxton. Meanwhile, he was bleeding all over his pants and Tori was about to have a conniption.

"Cade suffered a head wound during the accident, as well as a laceration on his leg," she said, worry stamped into her pale features. "How bad it is, we have no idea, since we haven't had a chance to tend it. He could very well bleed out while we sit here."

The younger one, who'd introduced himself as Deputy Avery, frowned. "Why don't I give you two a lift to the naval hospital on Lejeune? Or I can call an ambulance, if you'd rather."

"I don't need an ambulance," Cade told her. While his leg did hurt, he wasn't in agony.

Her relief evident, she gripped his hand and assisted him up. "We'll take you up on your offer."

As they passed through the gate manned by armed Marines, Cade should've felt safer. But their enemies were military and had the same access as he did. He was beginning to wonder if there was any place where he and Tori would be out of their reach.

It was almost 0300 hours by the time Claxton dropped them off at Cade's house. The deputy had met them in the ER department and stayed with Tori while Cade received treatment. The six-inch cut in his leg wasn't deep enough to cause major damage, but he hadn't been able to avoid stitches. His head wound was another story. He'd insisted on a butterfly bandage.

Claxton entered the house and, once the alarm was disarmed, cleared the rooms. He left with a promise to contact them the next day.

"You hungry?"

After removing his shoes, he padded into the kitchen and opened the fridge. Tori settled on one of the stools tucked along his island. Her hair was in disarray and her face smudged with dirt, but she'd never looked more beautiful.

"I could eat."

"I can make you a basic omelet or buttermilk pancakes. Or both."

She cocked her head to one side. "I'm in the mood for a sugar hit."

"Pancakes it is."

He set the ingredients on the counter. Tori joined him. "I'm not thinking straight. You should be resting your leg. I'll cook."

"The leg's fine. Barely a scratch."

She snatched the measuring cup from his hand. "You Marines and your pride." She sighed good-naturedly. "You'll have to settle for my help, then."

Cade smiled to himself. They'd done many things together, but cooking wasn't one of them. Should be interesting.

They didn't make small talk while they worked. Probably because they were both mentally rehashing the weekend's events.

When their plates were stacked high with pancakes, he topped them with whipped cream and powdered sugar. Tori poured the milk and arched a brow at him.

"I may not sleep after this."

"You might be surprised." He sat next to her at the island, liking the feeling of domesticity. "Remember, I have to be at my unit's headquarters bright and early. Until I get those leave papers signed, it's not official."

She drizzled maple syrup on the pancakes. "Tell me about your job?"

Pleased she'd expressed interest, he talked about his time in garrison, when he trained in and out of the classroom. He told her about deployments. Not the gut-wrenching stuff that sometimes kept him up at night. He told her what he could, which was even more than he'd told his parents.

Tori had that effect on him. Their friendship had united them like a two-person team on a life raft, navigating the perils of high school together.

She took a sip of milk. "It sounds like you've served alongside some wonderful people."

"I have."

He leaned over. "You have a milk mustache," he murmured, wiping the liquid with the pad of his thumb.

Tori swallowed hard. It felt like forever since she'd

looked at him like he was her favorite person in the world. His gaze lowered to her mouth, and his heart threatened to beat out of his chest.

What would she do if he kissed her?

She averted her face, giving him his answer. Not interested. Or not ready.

"You mentioned some guys in your platoon didn't agree with how you handled the incident with William. Could they be working with Aaron?"

"Corporal Wendell Lamont and Lance Corporal Rodney Truman. Both were close friends of his. I gave their names to Claxton tonight. He's going to work with the provost marshal on base. Check their recent whereabouts and see if there's a connection to Aaron."

"What exactly happened over there, Cade?"

Reliving that day in his head was hard enough. Saying the words aloud gave the events power, brought the smells, sounds, sights and emotions to life again. He preferred to keep them buried. Tori was entrenched in this mess, though.

"We were out on foot patrol, doing a walk-through of a town near the FOB."

Their heavy gear had made the oppressive heat almost unbearable. Dust had coated his skin. Little kids had trailed their group in anticipation, hoping for candy or snacks. "We were knocking on doors, talking with the locals, on the lookout for weapons caches or electronics that could be used as detonators."

"How many were in your group?"

"Twelve." Lamont, Truman and Poole had taken up the rear. Faulkner had been the closest to Cade. They'd left the last house on that street when Faulkner started mouthing off about his favorite sports team, taunting Lamont. "In my headset, I heard the warning of possible insurgents heading our way and orders to return to the FOB. Before I could instruct my men, a round whistled through the air and embedded in the wall near my head. We scrambled for cover."

Her hand covered his and held on tightly.

"Faulkner got shot in the leg. I dragged him behind a walled enclosure of the nearest house. He was losing too much blood, so I fashioned a tourniquet."

"While being fired upon?"

"We were pinned down by small arms fire. I radioed for the QRF. Sorry. That's the Quick Response Force."

"When did you learn about William?"

"I didn't see him get hit, but Lamont told us over comms. There wasn't anything we could do to try to save him."

He'd never forget that moment and the gut-punch realization that another Marine wasn't going to make it home to his family. William had been a good soul, a good Marine who'd given 100 percent of himself, both in training and in real-life battle. His had been a tougher-than-usual loss.

Cade had been devastated. He'd mourned William's death along with the rest of the men. He still wrestled with nightmares of that day. In wartime scenarios, a man in his position had to make split-second decisions. Did he second- and third-guess those decisions? Every day.

"I can't imagine," she murmured sadly. "How heart-wrenching for you and everyone there. Not to mention his friends and family."

He recalled their seething anger in the days following the ambush. They didn't accuse him within his hearing, but they also didn't try to hide their resentment. They were just shy of insubordinate. He'd ignored it because they'd been grieving. Reeling from the loss, like everyone in their platoon.

Thankfully, Brett had been there and offered a sounding board during those trying days.

"Lamont and Truman ignored the chain of command, went straight to my superior and complained that my actions led to William's death."

"That must've been difficult."

"To be honest, I didn't have too much time to dwell on their dissatisfaction. We continued with foot and mobile patrols. I had to keep my head in the game or risk another tragedy. The commanders did call us in one by one to record everyone's accounts of what transpired."

"And concluded that you weren't at fault."

"Yes." Regret weighed him down. "Not a day goes by that I don't wish we'd left even five minutes earlier. William would still be with us."

"Cade, Lamont and Truman suffered the loss of their friend. They blame you for his death. They could've joined forces with Aaron to enact revenge."

"It's possible. I'm afraid, until we find out, we're going to have be recluses. In the morning, we'll get my leave papers signed and then return here for the duration."

She forked another bite, soaking up the excess syrup on the plate. "An extended closure won't be good for The Canine Companion."

"You and your mom have a lot of loyal customers. They won't desert you."

"Fretting about my safety and the state of her business isn't going to help her reclaim her health." She put down her fork. "I thought coming home was a good idea. I prayed long and hard before handing in my resignation. I sought God's direction, but maybe I got it wrong."

Guilt stole his appetite. "I hate that you've been drawn

into this because of me." Pushing away his plate, he met her gaze. "With Claxton's help, we're going to identify the men working with Aaron. When we do, they'll be caught and thrown in jail."

"And if we don't figure it out in time?"

"I will do everything in my power to keep you safe, Tori."

Apprehension churned in her eyes. "What about you, Cade? Who's going to keep you safe?"

ELEVEN

Despite being on a guarded base among servicemen and women who knew how to handle emergencies and threats, Cade radiated unease. Beneath his blue T-shirt with the McMann fishing logo on it, his shoulders were taut with tension. Not knowing his enemies' identities and entertaining the possibility that it could be people he had worked closely with had to be tough to handle.

Tori couldn't imagine going into the library where she'd worked and worrying that one of her coworkers meant her harm.

They'd borrowed Jason's older sedan until they could get a rental. He and a friend had come to Cade's bright and early that morning to drop it off. The ride over to the main base had been a quiet one, both of them on the lookout for motorcycles. They both hoped no one would recognize them in the different vehicle.

Cade stuck close as they passed uniform redbrick buildings. His stride was shorter and slower than usual due to his leg wound. "As soon as we get my leave squared away, we'll go back to my place. Julian promised to drop off groceries later. You'll probably be bored, but you can finally rest and recuperate from our weekend's adventures."

"After what we've been through, I welcome the mundane."

They entered a huge, grassy field surrounded by more brick buildings—barracks where the younger men in Cade's infantry unit lived. There were offices, as well. Supply. Admin. Intel.

"This is the first time I've been on base in years. It's a hit of nostalgia."

She'd lived in base housing until the year she turned ten. Shortly after her birthday, her parents had decided to move to Sneads Ferry. They'd started attending the same church as the McManns, and a friendship between the families was born.

"The base theater's still there. Cheap movies and the best hotdogs you'll ever eat."

They shared a smile. Sometimes Tori missed the innocence of those days.

"We must've seen dozens of movies." Most of the time, it had been just her and Cade, but Angela had joined them on occasion.

"Hundreds," he countered, a twinkle in his eye.

Overhead, three helicopters buzzed toward the river. A loud boom rumbled beneath her feet. She flinched and shielded her head with her hands.

Cade's warm hands settled on her exposed shoulders. "It's okay. Just artillery practice."

Tori laughed at herself. "I forgot."

Camp Lejeune was a massive training area. People working and living on base quickly got used to the explosions, which could be felt from miles away.

Tori's attention wandered to a Marine near a set of brown dumpsters. His bright red hair caught her eye. Sunlight glinted off his glasses. He was leaning against one of the dumpsters, deep in conversation with a woman clothed in casual jeans and a shirt, a single ponytail trailing the middle of her back.

Tori latched onto Cade's hand and pointed. "Isn't that Heath?"

"He's supposed to be in class in half an hour."

The girl got up in Heath's face and jammed a finger in his chest. "That's not the same girl he had at Mom's party. What was her name? Looks like they're having a disagreement."

He shook his head. "You wouldn't believe some of the drama we have around here. It's like high school, only worse."

"Because of the frequent separations? And knowing someone you care about might be in harm's way?"

His somber gaze probed hers. "That adds to the strain, yes."

They watched as the girl stalked away, leaving Heath to stare after her.

"I hope he's not a poor influence on Jason," she mused.

"Seriously, Tori. You have to give your brother some credit."

She winced. "Even though he's eighteen, I still see him as my goofy little brother."

"He knows it, too."

"And resents it," she said with a sigh.

They cut a diagonal path across the field to the offices, which were located on the bottom level.

"Jason has a mom. He needs you to be his sister. A friend and confidante."

Cade was right. If she wanted to build a relationship with Jason, she had to start treating him like an adult.

He reached for the metal knob. "A word of warning. Having a female with me is going to blow their minds."

"Why is that? I have it on good authority that you

don't lack admirers." Admirers he kept at arm's length, she'd been told.

"My mom likes to think her only son is a catch." Rolling his eyes, he ushered her into a long room with painted cement-block walls and half a dozen metal desks. Men in camouflage and chunky sand-colored boots were busy with paperwork and phone calls. Tori felt their collective attention lock on to her, surprise reflected on their faces.

As Cade motioned her forward, the Marines offered friendly greetings and sly smiles that promised intense questioning later on. Not one of them impressed her as capable of personal vendettas. But she wasn't a good judge of character, was she?

He pointed out his desk. Besides the nameplate, there were no personal effects to set it apart from any other.

A blond man emerged from an office on their left. "Cade. What's this I hear about you taking emergency leave?"

"I'll fill you in later." He moved close, so that his shoulder pressed to hers. "Brett, I'd like you to meet Tori James."

The stripes on his sleeve indicated he was a staff sergeant, the same rank as Cade. The strip above his breast pocket announced his surname, Johnson. Slightly shorter than Cade, he had a stocky build and a pleasant demeanor. The pleasantness vanished at the mention of her name. His gaze cooled to ice chips and his lips lost their good humor.

"The ex-fiancée. Cade's told me about you." From the glint in his eyes, he didn't approve. Tori couldn't be sure if she was being paranoid or if he actually disliked her on sight. Indicating the sheaf of papers in his hand, he motioned to the door in back. "I'm taking these to Admin. Walk with me."

In the hallway, the fluorescent light glinted off black-and-white tiles that likely dated a few decades back. The building had a utilitarian vibe, but it was squeaky clean.

Walking in the middle, she glanced between the two men. "You were at Parris Island together?"

"A three-month long trial." Cade spoke first.

"I can think of a few other names for it." Brett nodded. "We were together again at SOI."

"School of Infantry?"

"Yes. We haven't always been in the same units, but we've kept in contact through the years." They turned a corner and proceeded along another nondescript hall. Brett cast her a sideways glance. "Cade told me you couldn't get out of North Carolina fast enough. What brought you back after all these years?"

Aware of Cade's frown, she said, "Business."

"Instead of family?" The condescension in his tone put her on the defensive. "You returned for financial gain instead of sentimental reasons."

"Excuse me?"

"It was a combination of both, actually." Cade stopped short, his hands clenched at his sides. "I don't know what's got under your skin, but Tori isn't on trial here."

"You're right," he said curtly. "Sorry."

"I've got papers to sign."

She and Cade retraced their steps. Just before turning the corner, Tori glanced over her shoulder. Brett stood, watching their retreat, anger evident in his locked jaw and stiff posture. Disquiet strummed through her. The staff sergeant's hostility had been instantaneous and, in her mind, unfounded.

Once Cade's business was squared away, she asked him about it.

"I apologize for his rudeness." They kept to the building's perimeter as they made their way to the parking lot. "While we were overseas, his wife got lonely and turned to another man." There was no denying his disgust. "I'd heard of it happening, of course, but not to anyone I knew."

At the sedan, he opened the door for her, a courteous habit he didn't think twice about.

"So he's angry with women in general?"

Cade stuck the key in the ignition but didn't start the engine. "He knows our history. I can only assume he was unhappy to see us together."

"How long ago did it happen?"

"She wrote him an email a couple of weeks before our tour was up, so a little more than six months ago."

Brett's heartbreak was fresh. No wonder he'd reacted the way he had. While their situations were different, Tori had left Cade. Just like Brett's wife had left him.

"An email? That's cold."

"She didn't have a choice. A mutual friend saw her out with the other man and threatened to tell Brett herself if she didn't. But yeah, it was harsh. He'd been stoked about their reunion. He was going to surprise her with a romantic getaway." He raked a hand through his hair. "He puts on a brave front, but he's not himself. He and Marlene were together for eight years. He expected to spend the rest of his life with her." He paused. "You know as well as I do that expectations aren't always realistic."

Tori stared out the window at a group of Marines sitting in a distant field, cleaning their weapons. "Angela warned me about spending time with you."

His hand fisted on his thigh. "Our friends are right to be concerned. We let our unresolved issues fester for ten years." His voice became strained. "We were planning a life together, Victoria. A house on the river, remember? A dog and three kids."

The loss of that dream punched her in the gut, as fresh as the day he told her the fateful news. "Of course I remember," she whispered.

"As far as I'm concerned, we both played a role in the demise of our relationship. I was an arrogant fool."

"What was I?"

He winced. "Hurt."

"I felt betrayed."

"You had every right to feel that way."

"But instead of staying and talking it out, I ran away."

"I'm sorry for every tear you shed because of me."

Her heart squeezed. "I'm sorry for not fighting for us."

His throat worked. "I propose a fresh start." Cade stuck out his hand. "What do you say? Friends again?"

Friendship with the man who'd captured her heart and never returned it? Was it possible? Or wishful thinking?

Tori placed her hand in his, praying she wasn't hurdling over a mental barrier that would spell her demise.

"Do you mind swinging by my apartment?" Tori asked as they left the base. "I'll need clothes and toiletries."

He checked the rearview mirror, on the lookout for anyone tailing them. "As long as we make it quick."

She'd had no choice but to wear the same black pants she'd had on last night. Her sparkly tank top had gotten torn in the scuffle, so he'd lent her a standard gray T-shirt with initials *USMC* in black across the front. It swallowed her petite form and hung to mid-thigh, but he liked seeing her in Marine gear. She'd combed her hair so that it fell in a shiny curtain around her cheeks.

The ride was uneventful. Jason's older model sedan was a good decoy. No doubt Aaron and his buddies would be expecting them to get a rental car. Not surprisingly, Jason had made them promise to replace it with a sports car if it got destroyed.

"Why does the sign say Open?" Tori scooted forward in the seat as they drew alongside the house. "And why is my mom's car in the driveway?"

"Knowing Barbara, she probably decided to man the shop alone."

"Without telling me?"

"You didn't tell her about our run-in in the woods."

"That's different," she huffed.

He parked on the curb behind a battered minivan and glanced around at the neighboring houses. So many hiding places.

"The way I see it, you're trying to shield her at the same time she's trying to prove she's not an invalid. You underestimate each other. You and Barbara are two of the strongest women I know."

Her eyes widened. "You think so?"

"Your mom launched and operated a business without the support of her husband." Whenever Thomas wasn't deployed, he'd chosen not to involve himself in his wife's venture. Another strike against him in Tori's book. "After his death, she carried on with the determination and discipline of a proper soldier. And you. Well, you were her second-in-command. Always there for her, whether it was helping Jason study for a test or manning the shop's cash register. Now look at you... You put your life on hold for her benefit and were rewarded with attacks on your life. Yet you didn't crumble. Didn't have a pity party. You're the epitome of grace under fire. If you were a Marine, I'd be fortunate to face the enemy with you by my side."

To his surprise, her eyes grew shiny with tears. "That's one of nicest things you've ever said to me."

She fumbled with the latch and let herself out of the car. Cade hurried around to her side, not sure whether to hug her or keep his distance. The main door opened, rattling the bell.

Barbara waved them over. "Come in. There's someone I'd like you to meet."

Inside the shop's front room, she introduced them to Felicia Ortiz and her cousin, Maria, who cradled a dark-eyed infant in her arms.

Tori's smile encompassed both women. "Felicia and I've met, but I haven't had the pleasure of meeting the woman responsible for these beautiful creations." She gestured to the hand-decorated dog cookies. "You're a talented lady. Our canine customers can attest to that."

"I enjoy what I do." Maria's brown eyes shone with pleasure. "Your mom has told me so much about you, Tori, that I feel as if I know you."

"I'm grateful Felicia has generously stepped in to keep your products stocked." Tori turned to Cade. "Felicia told me she was deployed at the same time as you. She was with the Female Engagement Team. Did you work with each other?"

He'd thought there was something vaguely familiar about her. FET members were few and far between. In a male-dominant country like Afghanistan, an FET was necessary to bridge communications between female locals and the military.

Felicia's pearl-white teeth flashed. "I can't say that I remember meeting you."

The baby squirmed and fussed. Felicia reached for him, held him against her shoulder and patted his tiny back.

Barbara shifted, giving him a glimpse of the framed photos beside the register. There were several of Barbara with Jason and Tori. The one that caught his eye was an older image of Tori and him, lounging on the front porch, Popsicles in their hands and goofy grins on their faces. Had Aaron come in the shop and seen the photo? It wouldn't have taken much to get Barbara to chat about her kids.

Barbara turned to Tori. "Since you can't be here right now, Felicia's agreed to be my part-time help. Isn't it wonderful? We won't have to disappoint our customers."

Tori's mixed feelings showed. "That's kind of you, Felicia, but what about your responsibilities on base?"

"I'm on terminal leave. I have thirty days of leave accrued."

"You're getting out of the Corps?"

The corners of her mouth turned down. "It was time."

A pair of customers arrived, a mother and her young daughter. They had their Siberian husky with them.

Cade drew Tori upstairs. "Time to pack."

She went into the bedroom and removed a duffel bag from the closet. "Is it safe for my mom to be here?"

He stationed himself by the window. "You're the target, Tori. Not her."

Her neighbor Kenneth emerged from his house with a bottle of lemonade. Sprawling onto a deck chair, he sipped the drink, his focus on Tori's house. Another man joined him. Scrawny, disheveled and dressed in leather and combat boots.

"What about Felicia?"

He shifted his attention to her. She slipped a pair of shorts from a hanger and folded them neatly.

"Like me, she's been trained to defend herself."

"She should know what she's getting into."

"Agreed."

Tori disappeared into the master bath. Drawers opened and closed. "We'll tell her before we leave?" she called.

Before he could respond, an unfamiliar number flashed on his cell.

Cade answered. It was his alarm company.

Tori must've heard the change in his voice, because she came to the bathroom door and waited for him to finish the call.

"Someone broke into your house?" Her eyes begged him to say no.

"The alert came three minutes ago. They've dispatched the authorities."

Tori tossed a smaller zippered bag into her duffel. "Let's go."

"You should stay here with your mom." He didn't want her anywhere near his house if Aaron or his cohorts were there.

She stalked over to him, angling her chin up to meet his gaze. "That wasn't the deal. Where you go, I go."

His chest grew tight with longing. "We're a team now, huh?"

"Until this is over, yes."

He wanted her safe, wanted the threat dealt with. What he didn't want was his time with her to end. Friendship with Tori was better than no relationship at all.

TWELVE

Julian was at Cade's house when they arrived fifteen minutes later. He'd been driving home for a long-awaited rest—his training schedule didn't always follow typical working hours—when Cade had texted him.

He'd been ordered to wait outside by the deputies, and he didn't look pleased. His nostrils flared, and his eyes grew flinty as he listened to Cade's account of last night's accident and subsequent confrontation.

He rubbed a hand along the short stubble shadowing his jaw. "That wouldn't have happened if I'd followed you home."

"You couldn't shirk your duties. Any idea when you'll leave town?"

Julian's brows lifted, and Cade nodded.

"Right. You couldn't say, even if you knew."

"Sorry, brother."

Their exchange reminded her of the times she'd come home from school and learned that her father had been called out of the country. Some days had been worse than others. Like birthdays celebrated without him. Piano recitals performed without him.

They may have had a tumultuous relationship, but that didn't mean she hadn't ached for her father long after his sacrifice. Or maybe she'd ached for another chance for the father-daughter relationship she'd dreamed of.

A pair of deputies exited the house and a third came around the side, having checked the fenced-in yard and surrounding property.

"There was no one here when we arrived, Mr. Mc-Mann. The alarm probably spooked them. Why don't you come inside and tell us if you see anything out of place or notice valuables missing?"

Cade and Tori entered first, followed by Julian and the others. The rooms looked the same as when they'd left that morning. The knowledge that their enemies had breached his home—their supposed safe house—set her nerves on edge.

Cade strode to the patio door, which was slightly ajar, and pointed to the overturned potted plant on the pavers. "Did one of you knock that over?"

"It was already like that." The deputy pointed out the handle. "Looks like they managed to get in by tampering with this lock."

His hands balled into fists. Cade was determined to protect her. This was further evidence their enemy was just as determined to get his hands on her. For what specific purpose, she couldn't bring herself to dwell on.

He methodically combed through the rest of the house. The deputies called for a member of the crime scene unit to come and dust for fingerprints. Two left to attend another call, leaving the third to wait in his cruiser outside.

Cade returned to the living room. "Aaron must've assumed we were home, considering neither of us has a vehicle at the moment."

Julian's gaze reflected his own misgivings. "You need a new place to stay. I'd offer you a spot in my apartment, but my sister's in from Hawaii. She'll be staying with me for another week."

Cade expelled a breath. "We need a place that isn't obviously connected to our friends and family."

"I thought you didn't want to stay in a hotel," Tori said.

"I don't if we can find an alternative." He snapped his fingers. "Brett's parents own a condo in Emerald Isle. It sits empty much of the year."

A beachside condo sounded too good to be true. Aaron wouldn't think to look for them among the summer tourist crowd. "Will he agree to help once he learns I'm involved?"

"As long as his parents are fine with the idea, he won't turn us down."

Cade stepped outside to place the call. Through the glass, she watched him reach to massage his wounded thigh and grimace. He was taking the prescribed antibiotics but refused pain medication, saying he needed to keep his mind sharp. A fresh bandage covered the gash on his temple, and the stitches in his arm peeked from beneath his T-shirt sleeve.

He'd received those wounds protecting her.

"No need to worry about him." Julian came to stand beside her, locking his hands behind his back. "He can handle that and much more."

"It's not that. What worries me is how far he's prepared to go."

Still speaking into the cell, he turned on the pavers and locked gazes with her, his expression fierce.

"He'll do whatever it takes to keep you safe," Julian said.

"Even if that means sacrificing his life?"

Julian's silent appraisal confirmed her fears.

"I can't let him do that."

"If it comes to that, it will be his choice to make."

Cade would give everything he had to defend her. He'd risk his life. He'd even die for her. He was the kind of man who would always put others' safety above his own.

Tori closed her eyes and sent a plea heavenward. *Please end this nightmare, Lord. Let us both walk out of this alive.*

Cade set the last of the supplies on the kitchen counter, his gaze drawn once again to Tori, who stood at the condo's sliding glass doors and contemplated the ocean. She'd been quieter than usual during the forty-five-minute drive to the small tourist island on the intracoastal waterway.

"You're armed, right?"

He turned to Julian, who waited with keys in hand. "I got my smaller gun back from the sheriff's department." He'd hit a taillight, not a person. "They're keeping my other one as evidence since I wounded Aaron with it. They'll return it at a later date."

"Good. Call or text anytime."

"Go home already, Tan." Julian should've hit the rack hours ago, but he'd insisted on following them up here and waiting with Tori while Cade ducked in an island market for food and other necessities. "Get some sleep."

Julian lowered his voice. "I know you have feelings for her, but don't allow emotions to cloud your judgment. Keep a cool head."

"Easy for you to say," he retorted, not bothering to deny the charge. "You've never let yourself care about a woman."

"Romance is too high-risk for me."

Cade rolled his eyes. There wasn't much that could

spook the Force Recon Marine, so why he avoided serious-minded women like the plague was a mystery.

After locking the door behind his friend, he walked through the living room and rejoined Tori. She looked like a tourist. Her ankle-length dress, with its soft mint-green, pink and white pattern, paired with strappy sandals, screamed lazy days in the sun. Thin straps showed off her smooth shoulders and arms. She wore no makeup save for a coral-hued lip gloss, making her look years younger, reminding him of the girl he'd fallen hard for.

Beyond the small patio, sunlight glinted off azure water stretching to the horizon. Dense shrubbery separated the units from the parking lots.

She gave him a half-hearted smile that didn't quite reach her eyes.

"What are you thinking about?"

"The times our families went camping together." Nodding to the gaggle of kids catching tiny crabs at the water's edge, she said wistfully, "Remember when we used to do that?"

"I remember being unable to sleep in the tent because it was too humid, but my dad wouldn't let me sleep outside because of alligators."

The base's camping site was located on a thin stretch of land between the ocean and river, and alligators had been spotted in the area.

A sparkle lit in her eyes. "We used to have contests—"

"To see who could build the biggest s'mores tower."

"I won nine times out of ten."

"Because I let you."

Out of the corner of his eye, sudden movement had him reaching for Tori to push her behind him. But it was just a girl of about eight, fetching her beach ball.

"We shouldn't stand in the open."

The sparkled faded. "Right."

Tori moved aside so Cade could pull the curtains closed, blocking the stunning view. They were safer in this condo than any other place he could think of. Only a handful of people knew their exact location. Brett and his parents, of course, along with Julian, Deputy Claxton and Jason.

Hating that he'd had to spoil her mood, he went to the closet and pulled out a stack of dusty boxes.

"You up for a round of Pay Day? Or do you prefer Monopoly?"

She sank onto the love seat and pretended to debate her choices. "I was the Pay Day champion. Let's see if your skills have improved."

Snagging a flat decorative pillow, he dropped it onto the carpet on the opposite side of the coffee table. "Again, because I let you win."

She dragged the box over and laid out the pieces. "You have a faulty memory, Staff Sergeant."

"We'll see about that."

Halfway through the game, she cupped the red die in her hands but didn't roll it.

"Why are you still single?"

A choked laugh escaped. "Where did that come from?"

"You don't think your mother has kept my mother informed of your dating habits through the years? And that my mother didn't pass that info along to me?"

He shifted on the pillow, hiding a grimace at the dull throbbing in his thigh. "What did they tell you?"

"That you keep women at arm's length." Propping her elbow on the glass top, she rested her cheek in her hand. A casual pose, yet her eyes swam with curiosity. "You were ready to get married at eighteen. I was convinced you'd find someone and settle down within a few years."

"I thought I would, too. I concentrated on my career at first. By the time I was ready to date, I started noticing the crumbling of too many marriages. Granted, some were doomed from the beginning, naive, immature people marrying on a whim without serious thought to the hard work and sacrifice it would require. Brett's experience gave me serious misgivings. If anyone was going to make it, it would've been Brett and Marlene."

Her brow puckered. "You used to be the optimistic one."

"And you, the realist." He lined the deal cards in a neat row beside the board. "About Patrick... You never answered my question."

Her lashes sweeping down, she toyed with the die. "Our relationship wasn't a love story for the ages. We had fun together. We bowled in the summer and ice-skated in the winter. Ate our weight in barbecue. Funny, I didn't realize until after he went to jail that we'd rarely spent time alone, certainly not enough to build a solid foundation on."

Cade was ashamed of the jealousy her words evoked. Somehow, spending the past few days in her company had made the idea of her with another man more difficult to swallow.

"But the breakup hurt you."

Her father had been the first to instill distrust in Tori. Cade had been the second, when he'd embarked on a new—and binding—career path without consulting her. Patrick had compounded the problem. Tori would have trouble forgiving herself for not seeing the signs.

"Because I allowed myself to be fooled by him."

He blew out a breath. "You can't blame yourself. People with secrets can be masters at hiding their true agendas."

"Maybe."

He received a call from Claxton, preventing him from arguing the point. Tori sat up straight and listened to his side of the conversation.

"A homemade explosive device was used to blow up my car," she said when he'd pressed End.

He nodded. "Aaron and his buddies had to have a working knowledge of explosives and the means to obtain the C-4. These days, you can find specific instructions on the internet."

"This doesn't help us identify who he's working with."

"Claxton's going to work with the Provost Marshal's Office on several fronts. They're looking to see if there have been reports of missing explosives on base. They're also going to dig into the lives of the two Marines who lodged the complaint over in Afghanistan. Lamont's married and living in base housing on Tarawa Terrace. Truman lives in the barracks."

Abandoning the game, Tori got up and paced to the window facing the parking lot. The curtains were drawn, however, so she faced the room.

"You served with them. Do you think they're guilty?"

He slowly stood to his feet. "Lamont can be a hothead, but he's also a family man. He carried around a photo of his wife and sons and talked about them incessantly. I can't see him jeopardizing their future. Truman, on the other hand, is a wild card. He was the last one I'd expect to play the blame game."

"He's single, since he's living in the barracks. Does he have a girlfriend? Kids from a previous relationship?"

"No kids. No romantic ties that I'm aware of."

"Which means he has less to lose."

"We know Aaron's motivation. He said that he and William were like brothers. As for the others, their involvement could boil down to a hefty payday."

"Aaron would need access to a lot of cash," she mused, hugging her middle. "We know he didn't get rich on military pay. Claxton should look into whether he comes from a wealthy family. Or if illegal activity is cushioning his accounts."

"It doesn't have to be about money," Cade said. "Aaron could have dirt on the others and is coercing them."

She rubbed her hands down her face. "Speculation isn't going to get us out of hiding."

"Tired of my company already? It hasn't even been an hour."

"We can't stay here indefinitely." She spread her hands. "You have to go back to work, and so do I. Felicia isn't working for free."

"Trust me, I wish we could be out there searching for answers, too. But until we put faces on every one of these guys, we have to stay out of sight."

"It angers me that he's manipulated us into putting our lives on hold."

Cade wondered what frustrated her more. Being isolated in a hideout for an unknown amount of time or being isolated with *him*. Despite their agreement to start fresh, tension swirled below the surface. He was still attracted to her, and he was positive she felt the same pull.

"It won't last forever."

"I know." Her teeth sunk into her full bottom lip. Looping her duffel bag over her arm, she inclined her head toward the stairs. "I'm going to take my stuff to my room. Maybe read a book."

They'd agreed he'd take the first-floor bedroom and that she'd have the second-floor area to herself.

Cade hid his disappointment. He'd anticipated spending the next few hours with her, reconnecting over shared memories and a childhood board game.

Her foot was on the bottom step when she stopped and changed directions. Skirting the dining table and chairs, she went to the short bar-style counter separating the eating area from the kitchen and pulled a large knife from its wooden holder.

"You have your Beretta. I'll keep this on my nightstand."

He didn't mention all the ways that knife could be used against her, especially considering Aaron's military training. If having it in her room helped her sleep better, so be it. Cade wasn't going to let anyone get to her.

THIRTEEN

Tori hadn't been asleep long when a noise woke her. It took her a few seconds to recognize the rattan furniture and tropics-inspired ceiling fan. This was her fourth night at the condo. Since she hadn't left the confines of these walls, she should be used to these surroundings by now.

Pushing upward to rest against the headboard, she listened for unusual sounds and failed to detect anything that would be cause for alarm. Her window was above a portion of the parking lot, and sometimes the slamming of car doors or loud conversations would leach through it. That was mostly during the day, though.

Right before she'd gone to bed, Cade had mentioned he had another half hour before his show ended. A quick glance at the nightstand told her more than an hour had passed. He was probably snoozing already.

She thrust the covers aside. Because of the circumstances, she'd opted against her usual pajama short set and chosen to wear a soft T-shirt and loose cotton pants to bed. She picked up the knife and trudged to the door. Sleeping wouldn't be an option until she reassured herself the windows and doors were locked tight.

Or maybe you're hoping to share a midnight snack with your gorgeous ex-fiancé?

Being cooped up with Cade had her traversing an emotional tightrope. It amazed her how quickly they'd fallen into old patterns, teasing and challenging each other, working as a typical couple when it came to meals and cleanup. Like the boy she'd adored, the grownup Cade was witty and, at times, insufferably obstinate. But considerate and committed to making this time of isolation bearable for her.

Beyond her door, thick silence greeted her. Cade was probably asleep. The light from her room created a thin shaft on the stairs, and she descended into the dark lower floor, the carpet soft and cool against her bare feet.

In the small foyer, she reached for the doorknob and went still. Something felt off.

Squeezing the knife handle until it dug into her palm, she peered into the living area and kitchen. The shadows were complete, thanks to the drawn blinds and curtains. The area where the couches and entertainment center were situated was inky black. Her heart pounded in her ears as she crept toward the kitchen. When the curtain billowed and a briny breeze wafted through the condo, Tori realized she was hearing the waves hitting the surf.

The sliding glass door was open.

Please, let it be Cade outside, moon gazing.

Hugging the wall on her left, she inched along the smooth surface, intent on reaching Cade's room. Maybe he'd heard the same noise that had disturbed her. Or maybe he'd planned to go outside and gotten a phone call, but his phone was in his room.

Her overactive brain ran through various scenarios.

Bottom line, Cade wouldn't have left them vulnerable to attack. No matter that they'd been here since Monday without incident and their location was known to a few select people.

As she neared the hallway, the sense of foreboding enveloped her.

Knots formed below her sternum. Her palms grew sweaty.

Offering up a prayer for protection, she whipped around the corner and tripped over something in the open doorway. Gasping, she bumped into the wall, using it to keep her upright.

She fumbled for the light switch. A scream ripped from her lips at the sight that greeted her. The knife clinked onto the tiles.

"Cade!" Dropping down beside his prone form, she struggled to turn him onto his back. "Please be okay," she repeated again and again.

Still dressed in his T-shirt and pants, he had no visible injuries. No new ones, anyway. But his eyes were closed, his mouth slack.

She pressed her fingers to his neck. A pulse. He had a pulse.

The scrape of a shoe against the tiles behind her warned her she wasn't alone. Too late. A body slammed into her, shoving her to her stomach. Her cheek glanced off the hard floor, pain ricocheting through her skull. She tried to crawl out of reach. Failed.

His knee hit her mid-back and pinned her in place.

Cold terror shafted through her. *The next time you see her, she'll be in pieces.*

That's what Aaron had said.

Gloved hands wrapped around her throat and squeezed. Hot breath scalded her ear.

This wasn't Aaron, her dazed mind realized. No smell of smoke. And he was lighter. Not as stocky. The masked man from the woods?

Tori maneuvered her left hand to try to pry his fingers

away. He increased the pressure, bruising the sensitive skin and cutting off her air supply. His complete silence was horrifying.

He was going to wait until she was unconscious and transport her to another location. Unless the plan had changed and the decision was made to kill her first and then move her lifeless body.

Fight, Tori! Fight!

She squirmed and kicked. She wasn't going to make this easy for him.

But he was stronger and in a position of control.

The knife!

With her right hand, she swiped the floor in a wide arc. Her fingertips brushed against metal. There. If she could scoot just an inch closer to Cade, she could grab it.

Black dots danced before her eyes. Time was running out. Her lungs felt like they were going to burst.

Somehow, she managed a weak grip on the weapon. Summoning all her strength, she twisted her head and jabbed the blade into his leg.

An anguished hiss blew through her hair. The second his grip loosened, she slammed her head back against his nose and shimmied from beneath him. Gulping in air, she stumbled to her feet. Her attacker was between her and the exit.

She dashed into another bedroom and slammed the door closed. Before she could lock it, he shouldered it open.

Tori backed away, searching the room for a makeshift weapon. There was none. Besides, he had the knife in his hand.

Her heels encountered the baseboard between the dresser and nightstand. Nowhere else to go.

He stopped by the foot of the bed and glared at her, chest heaving, blood dripping from the tear in his pants.

Unnerved, Tori experienced a rush of anger. "Why won't you speak? Your boss likes to gloat and taunt. Not you." Her fingers dug into the Sheetrock. "You haven't made a peep."

She sensed rather than saw his scowl. Then a thought hit her.

"I know you," she breathed. "I know you, and that's why you haven't spoken. Because you're afraid I might recognize your voice."

He grunted and lifted the weapon. Took a step in her direction.

Out of options, Tori began to beat on the wall and scream as loudly as she could manage. The units shared common walls. It was late. Someone had to be sleeping on the other side. If she could wake them—

"Tori!"

Cade. She spun around, fully expecting to find her attacker about to pounce.

He was gone.

Tori bolted into the hallway in time to see him flee through the open patio door. Cade was using the door-jambs to leverage himself up.

"What happened?"

She rushed past him and secured the door with shaky fingers. Then she returned to his side and, looping an arm around his ribs, assisted him to the couch.

"I heard something. Found you passed out." Sitting so that there wasn't even an inch separating them, she let her hands roam over his face, his shoulders and arms. "Do you remember anything?"

"I was preparing to turn in when I heard a noise. I went to investigate. That's it." He raked his hand through his hair and, wincing, came away with traces of blood on his fingers.

Tori carefully explored his head and located a sizable lump. "He knocked you over the head with something."

"Raising a commotion was smart thinking. Considering the amount of people occupying these units and milling about the grounds, he had to have counted on rendering you unconscious before moving you."

"The walls aren't soundproof," she said. "I'd hoped to rouse someone's attention."

Pounding on the front door startled her.

Cade's eyes shot to hers. "Looks like you succeeded." He pushed himself off the cushions and trudged to the door.

"Is everything okay in there?" a male voice boomed.

Cade peeked through the peephole. "Don't recognize him."

On the other side of the door, a big, barrel-shaped man with a beard stood in nothing but a pair of swim trunks and sandals. A woman waited behind him wearing a bathrobe. Their eyes widened at the sight of Tori. Of their own volition, her fingers touched her throbbing cheek.

"Do you need me to call the police, miss?" The man cast a hard glare at Cade. "You can wait in our condo until they arrive."

At his implication, she rushed out, "Oh, no, this isn't what you think. We had an intruder."

The woman gripped her husband's arm. "The kids are asleep. If there's someone breaking into the units, we shouldn't leave them alone."

Tori slipped her hand in Cade's. "Thank you for coming to check on us. I wasn't sure if there was anyone on the other side of the wall."

He looked Tori in the eye. "You need us, just holler."

When they'd gone, Cade shut and locked the door. Then he turned to her.

Smoothing a wayward lock of hair behind her ear, he cupped her jaw and brushed his thumb lightly across her throbbing cheek. Fury built in his eyes, darkening them to almost black.

"We have to call Claxton. Get a team up here to go through this place with a fine-tooth comb. We're going to identify this guy and everyone else in Aaron's circle. And then they're going to pay for hurting you."

"Not yet." Her body began to shake. "I need for you to hold me."

Cade gingerly traced the purplish-yellow marks on her slender neck, again reliving the helplessness he'd felt when he'd regained consciousness to the sound of her screams. Helplessness that had given way to anger. Anger at himself for failing her. Anger at Aaron and the beasts doing his bidding.

Need sprung to life in her eyes. Her lips quivered.

"When is this going to stop? What if the next time is the time he gets it right?"

Cade pulled her close. Curling into him, she rested her cheek against his chest and hugged his waist. His heart raced at the same frantic pace as the night of senior prom, when he'd finally admitted his feelings and kissed her for the first time. Not since Tori had he experienced a connection like this. A deep, emotional bond forged by friendship.

He stroked her hair, reveling in her complete surrender, her willingness to lean on him.

"We have to remember God's in control," he murmured, more for himself than her. "He has a plan."

Her arms tightened. "For the life of me, I can't see any reason for such a plan."

"I know." He brushed a kiss to her temple, ignoring the dull ache in his skull. "It's hard to trust Him when we're in the middle of a storm."

"How did you do it? When you were in Afghanistan?"

"I kept repeating a verse I learned years ago. 'For without faith, it's impossible to please God.'"

Cade didn't always like or understand the ways of His Creator. He couldn't fathom why an upstanding guy like William Poole had to lose his life or why a kind-hearted, generous woman like Tori would be targeted. But he believed God was all-knowing and all-powerful. He believed God loved people and wanted a relationship with them.

"'His thoughts are above our thoughts, His ways above our ways,'" she softly quoted.

Cade didn't stand a chance against the need swamping him. Tipping up her chin, he gazed deep into her eyes, searching for answers to questions he dared not give voice to. She looked lost. He yearned to take away her anguish. When her fingers curled into his sides and she snuggled closer, he dipped his head and slanted his mouth over hers. Her lips were as soft and welcoming as he remembered. She clung to him, returning his kiss.

The woman she'd become fascinated him. He wanted to know more, to know everything she was willing to share.

The chemistry that had always simmered between them roared to life, temporarily blocking out their surroundings. His world centered on her. Victoria Elaine James. The only woman he'd ever envisioned a future with. For a few brief, blissful moments, she was his again. Nothing stood between them.

Tori abruptly ended the embrace, pulling away and hugging her arms around her middle, as if she required protection from him.

"Has nothing changed?" he said, already aware of the answer.

A battle waged in her eyes. "I respect you, Cade. I admire what you stand for, what you fight for."

"But you want nothing to do with the type of life I lead."

"I'm sorry." She threaded her hair out of her face with trembling hands. "I can't make decisions about us right now."

Cade's initial reaction was hurt, followed by disappointment. He tamped them down. Ten years ago, he'd made the mistake of being rash. He'd learned the value of patience since then.

"Understood."

Anguish twisted her mouth. "The last thing I want is to hurt you again."

"I shouldn't have pressed you. Probably shouldn't have kissed you, given our current emotional states."

"Right. This wouldn't have happened if not for the danger we've found ourselves in."

Cade pressed his lips together to restrain the argument building inside. He wasn't sure he agreed with her assessment. But it wasn't the time or the place.

"Whatever the case," he finally said, "we have bigger problems to focus on."

They could determine the significance of that kiss later.

He prayed there would be a later. His enemies weren't going to stop until they were apprehended or he and Tori were dead.

FOURTEEN

"I don't think there's any damage to the condo," Cade said. "If you notice anything I missed, I'll cover the cost to fix it."

Brett sprawled in one of the metal patio chairs, fingers clutching the armrests and his knees bouncing. He'd insisted on coming when Cade had called. "I thought no one would find out about this place."

"That's what we assumed, too."

The curtains had been drawn, and all the lights inside were on. Through the glass, he could see Emerald Isle police officers milling around. Tori was in deep conversation with her brother, Jason. Fatigue bracketed her mouth, and her shoulders were curved inward, her fingers periodically touching the bruises on her throat.

He mentally kicked himself again for giving his emotions free reign. Kissing her hadn't been the wisest thing to do, not when they were both distracted and on edge.

"And you said your Jeep's a total loss?"

Cade shifted against the patio's low concrete barrier. "There's no saving it."

He'd poured time, energy and money into modifying the vehicle. He regularly scoured online forums for the latest information and had joined a local club that went off-roading on weekends. His friends had teased him about never being satisfied with it. They didn't know Jeep stood for Just Empty Every Pocket.

"That girl isn't worth the trouble." Brett's mouth became an irate slash.

"None of this is Tori's fault." Cade worked to contain his annoyance. "She was dragged into this in order to punish me."

His knees stopped bobbing. "What?"

"I haven't had a chance to update you, I guess. Aaron let it slip that he's avenging William Poole's death. Hurting her is a means to an end."

"Before he kills you, you mean. Stands to reason that if Tori had stayed in Knoxville, none of this would've happened. Your life was normal before she came around."

His head throbbed. "How did you know she lived in Knoxville?"

His brows crashed together. "You told me."

"I told you she was in Tennessee. I didn't mention what city. Furthermore, you're the *only* person I confided in about her."

"I don't run my mouth," Brett said with a grunt. Then his eyes widened, and he jammed his thumb against his chest. "Hold on, you don't think that I'm involved…"

Cade pinched the bridge of his nose, fighting fatigue and confusion. "No, of course not."

Brett came over, gripped his shoulders and gave him a little shake.

"You're like a brother to me," Brett squeezed out, hurt wrestling with anger. "Family."

Their shared experiences and confidences had formed a strong friendship. "I'm desperate for answers, that's all."

"And I'm just trying to look out for you."

"Tori's not the enemy."

Releasing him, Brett shook his head. "She inspired this revenge plot. Send her away. At least until you get answers."

"She doesn't take orders from me."

"Use your powers of persuasion."

"No."

"You're making a mistake."

"You're letting your grief and battered pride skew your thinking. If you don't deal with what Marlene did to you, it'll eat you from the inside out."

His head reared back. "You're one to talk. You're acting as if your ex-fiancée didn't stomp all over you. Makes me sick how you cater to her, while she acts like an innocent hothouse flower."

Cade gritted his teeth, trying to hold in words he might regret. The door slid open, and Jason sauntered outside. Brett stalked to the corner and took up a position beside the grill.

"Am I interrupting something?"

"No," Cade said, blanking his face. "Learn anything new?"

"Not yet. Tori's talking to Deputy Claxton now." He stared out at the black night and moonlight glancing off the sea, his expression troubled. "I know you both think I let it slip, the fact that you were hiding out here. But I promise I kept my mouth shut. My mom couldn't even get me to squeal."

"We believe you, Jason."

"They're going to test the blood on the knife, but it will take days. Maybe weeks."

No one spoke for a few minutes. He and Tori didn't have the luxury of time.

"Brett, you were around when William died," Cade said. "Can you think of anyone who acted out of the ordinary?"

"Besides Lamont and Truman?" His brows descended. "Not off the top of my head. William was well-liked. The type of guy who didn't make enemies. Everyone was sad about it."

"Yeah, but who was torn up enough to target me?"

Grief was powerful and overwhelming. Instead of dealing with the complex emotions, some people suppressed them. Apparently, Aaron's thought processes had been warped before the death of his friend, and he'd crossed into lunacy. Question was, whom had he dragged along with him?

"I don't know." Brett shrugged.

Cade began to pace. "We've been home six months. Has anyone in the platoon acted strangely? Maybe someone who's had a change in behavior or personality?"

Brett's arms dropped to his sides. "I don't know why I didn't think of it before."

"What?"

"Who used to be a model Marine but has spent multiple weekends on fire watch?"

In the early years, Cade had been assigned to fire watch one or two times for minor mess-ups. Walking around the barracks picking up trash while his buddies relaxed hadn't been fun. He mentally reviewed the list of the men under his command and stopped short. "Heath Polanski."

Jason's head jerked back. "Heath would never do anything to hurt my sister."

"I haven't heard him mention William," Cade said, reluctant to jump to conclusions. "But his performance hasn't matched his pre-deployment levels."

"Neither has his attitude. He's gotten into at least two physical altercations with other Marines," Brett inserted.

"No. You're wrong."

Cade sighed. "Jason, we have to explore every angle. How long ago did you start hanging around him?"

"I don't know. Maybe two months."

"So you don't know him well enough to be sure," Brett said.

"Sure about what?" Tori stepped through the door.

The three of them regarded her in silence. Her frown deepened.

"Someone tell me what's going on."

Jason threw his arms wide. "They think I've made friends with a murderer."

Her green eyes shot to Cade. "What's he talking about?"

"Heath Polanski."

"You think Heath was with us in the woods? And that he came here tonight…" Her gaze dropped to the ground.

Cade took a step closer. "What are you thinking?"

"I…" Her teeth sank into her lower lip. "He weighed less than Aaron. Taller and leaner."

"And that's enough to pin this on him?" Jason demanded.

She began to twist the ring around her finger. "His complete silence struck me as odd, especially after Aaron's chatter. I assumed the reason he refused to speak was because he didn't want me to recognize him. I even told him so. But there are no specific details that would make me think it's him. Besides, Heath wears glasses. This guy didn't."

"He could have prescription contacts," Brett pointed out.

Cade placed his hand on Jason's shoulder. "I know you

want to defend your friend, but it's worth a look into a possible connection. For your sister's sake."

He looked as if he would protest more, but his gaze lit on Tori. He nodded.

"Don't tip him off," Brett warned.

Jason's only response was a tightening of his jaw.

Cade extracted the keys from his pocket. "I'm going to have a talk with Heath."

"Now?" Tori said. "It's after midnight."

"Which means he's supposed to be in the barracks. Best time to pay him a visit."

"I'm going with you," Jason announced.

"It's better that you don't," Cade told him. "Why don't you keep Tori company until I get back?"

Her chin jutted. "You're not leaving me behind."

Cade's first instinct was to point out that she needed rest after tonight's ordeal. But he had the feeling she'd fight him. To be honest, he'd worry less having her with him. They'd be on base, in the barracks, surrounded by dozens of Marines.

"I don't have the energy to argue the issue," he said at last.

At once, her expression changed. "You should've let Claxton call the ambulance. Is your head still paining you? What about your leg?"

"The leg's fine, and I can handle a simple headache," Cade said. "No hospitals."

"Then I'm driving. Hand over the keys."

Deputy Claxton chose that moment to join them. He held up a tiny device.

"We found a tracker on Jason's car."

Jason's eyes hardened as a war played over his face. He turned to Cade. "Call me as soon as you find him. I want to know whether or not I let a psycho get close to my sister."

* * *

They passed the sign indicating they were nearing Camp Lejeune's main gate. Light from the streetlamps flashed through the windows, illuminating Tori's tight grip on the steering wheel and the tension in her face. Cade resisted the urge to reassure her with a touch. Something about her demeanor sent out a clear message: *stay away.*

He recognized that she was a civilian who, like most people, went about her daily life unaware of the underbelly of criminal activity. She'd coped well with everything that had happened, but there was only so much a person could take before the constant fear and anxiety overwhelmed them.

He wanted to be her protector. Her shelter. Her strength.

He couldn't do that if she shut him out.

God, I need a little insight here. You put me in a position to help her, to be a friend. I can't be what she needs without You guiding me.

"We should talk about what happened at the condo."

"There's no need to rehash it. We've told the police everything."

"I meant what happened between us."

Her gaze never leaving the road, she said, "We agreed to set our personal issues aside, did we not?"

"I just don't want you to worry about a repeat performance. I won't lie and say I'm not drawn to you. That hasn't changed in ten years, and I can't see it ever changing." At her quick sideways glance, he said, "That being said, I can and will control it. I won't do anything to jeopardize the trust you've placed in me."

Instead of passing through the main gate, she parked in the visitors' area, where they'd have to obtain a pass since Jason's car didn't have a base sticker and she didn't have a military ID.

Resting her hands in her lap, she angled toward him. "I trust you, Cade. You've done nothing to make me question your commitment to my well-being." She heaved a sigh. "We were once engaged. It's to be expected that the connection we once shared, the romantic feelings we had for each other, would return. *That's* what we can't trust." She gestured between them. "We're in a fight for our lives. Emotions are heightened. That kiss was simply the fallout from our close proximity and near-death experiences. It didn't mean anything."

Cade forced his gaze elsewhere so she wouldn't see the *fallout* from her words. For him, that kiss had meant something. It meant that everything he'd told himself the past ten years was a lie. He wasn't over Tori. Not by a long shot.

"You're right." Wrestling with what felt like fresh rejection, he projected a calm he didn't feel. "I don't know why I brought it up."

Opening the car door, he got out into the humid night and walked with her to the building, pretending not to notice the frequent furtive looks she sent him. After obtaining the pass, Tori drove them past the commissary, library and various fast-food restaurants to the unit's barracks.

Most of the rooms were dark. PT came early.

"I don't see his truck." He pointed to a window on the third floor. "He shares a room with Dante Murray. Looks like he's still up. Let's go see if Heath's roommate can shed some light on his recent behavior troubles."

They climbed the outdoor stairs and continued along the breezeway. Cade knocked on the door. Music came from a television or other device. "Murray, you in there?"

The door swung open. "What do you want—" His eyes bulged. "Staff Sergeant McMann."

"My friend, Miss James, and I have a couple of questions to ask you."

"Yes, sir." Hurrying to mute the television, he backed against his twin bed. "What can I do for you, sir?"

Tori glanced around the room that resembled a college dorm. There were two of everything—narrow beds, desks, wooden desk chairs and cushioned chairs. A bathroom was situated against the rear wall.

Cade closed the door and gestured to the empty bed opposite Dante's. "Where's Heath?"

"I don't know, sir. He left hours ago."

"Didn't say where he was headed?" Cade wandered to Heath's desk. There wasn't much in the way of personal items. A packet of unopened MCIs—curriculum that must be completed for Heath to advance in rank. A nondescript lamp. A red plastic cup filled with pens and a pair of scissors. A laptop.

"No, sir."

Tori nodded to the calendar taped to the cement wall. "He likes *Star Wars*."

"Doesn't everyone?" Cade murmured.

"Is he in some kind of trouble?" Dante ventured.

"That's what we're trying to figure out," Cade said. "He's been displaying troubling behavior. You and he have roomed together for almost a year. Have you noticed any changes in his hobbies or friends? Sleeping or eating habits?"

Hesitating, he licked his lips and glanced at the television screen.

"We want to make sure he's not involved in something dangerous."

He did a double take. "Dangerous? Heath?"

Cade crossed his arms and waited.

Dante sank onto the bed and steepled his hands. "He's been torn up since the deployment. He's different. Quiet. Restless."

Tori bent to examine a Jedi alarm clock on the headboard shelves. "What was he like before?"

"Fun to be around. Sometimes too chatty."

"Have you asked him about it?" Cade said.

"He insists he has nothing to say." He frowned. "It's like sharing a room with a robot."

Cade noticed a corkboard above Dante's bed. It was almost completely covered with photos of Dante with his Marine buddies and probably family members. Heath's side was a blank canvas. "Heath doesn't have any personal pictures?"

Dante's gaze swept the opposite walls. "He used to have a couple posters and a few framed pictures, but he took them down."

"When?"

"A week or two ago, I think."

Tori shot him a worried look. The timing was suspect. Was he trying to hide something? Maybe a connection to the attempts on their lives?

Cade was tempted to rifle through his belongings, but he didn't want to jeopardize the investigation. Best to get the MPs in here.

"Did you know any of the people in the pictures?"

"I didn't really pay attention," he said, apologetic. "Since William's death, he's become a loner. But he does go into town a lot. I don't know who he sees or where he goes. I asked once or twice, and he got snarly."

Definitely suspicious.

"Thanks for your help," Cade said. "If you think of anything else, let me know."

Dante bolted to his feet. "Yes, Staff Sergeant."

Cade opened the door and scanned the parking lot below. "And it would be best if you didn't mention our visit."

"Understood, sir."

If they weren't both exhausted, he'd suggest they wait around for him to show. Instead, they returned to the car and drove through the deserted streets. In the passenger seat, Cade mulled over what they'd gleaned from Dante, not really focused on the passing scenery. This section of the base consisted of long, rectangular brick buildings. Warehouses for various units.

"Stop."

Tori applied the brakes, slowing their speed. "What's up?"

"See that truck? Looks like Heath's."

She guided the sedan off the road and was heading between two buildings when a tall, lanky figure walked around the corner.

"Did you see that?" Cade reached for the handle. "He's limping."

As soon as the car stopped, he jumped out. His prey noticed he had company and bolted back the way he'd come.

Cade gave chase, his only thought to capture this guy and get answers by any means possible.

FIFTEEN

Before Tori had a chance to voice a warning or demand he wait for her, Cade had hauled himself onto the warehouse's shoulder-high walkway and disappeared from sight. Jittery with nerves, she angled the car next to the building and jerked the keys from the ignition before sprinting after him. She took the concrete ramp up to the walkway and searched the darkness.

No fading footsteps to guide her. No shouts.

Where had he gone?

As her eyes adjusted, she could just make out the outline of a door in the brick facade. It was ajar. In the opening, she peeked inside, her instincts jangling a warning. The glow of a computer monitor emitted enough light to see the metal desk on which it sat and nothing more.

Tori said a prayer and tiptoed inside.

A hand clamped on to her shoulder and spun her toward the wall. An involuntary gasp escaped before she recognized Cade's scent.

"You should've waited in the car," he whisper-growled in her ear.

"I'd rather be in here with you than alone out there," she retorted. "You watch my back. I watch yours."

His sigh gusted over her cheek. "Stay close."

Latching onto her hand, he drew her along the rough-textured wall until they reached metal shelving. While she couldn't make out particulars, she sensed that they extended high above her head.

"What is this place?" she murmured.

"CIF. Consolidated Issue Facility." A beat later, he whispered, "They issue our gear here."

They reached a wide, central aisle. Cade released her hand as he rounded the unit first, his big body an obstacle between her and their enemy. One by one, they passed the rows crowded with cardboard boxes. The huge, dark warehouse sat like a silent tomb. Tori's throat closed in, and her legs didn't want to obey her mind's order to move forward.

Was Heath working with Aaron?

Had Aaron somehow gotten through base security and was here to meet Heath and plot their next step?

Suddenly, twin lights clicked on, blinding them. An engine thundered to life. The high-pitched grind of metal forks rising froze her in her tracks. The forklift jerked into motion.

"Look out!" Cade seized her. Propelled her to the right, between the shelves.

Tori stumbled to the concrete. He hauled her back up and urged her to run.

Behind them, the forklift was executing the turn. The thick wall loomed ahead. He was going to pin them in. Then what? Skewer them to the wall with those metal prongs?

"Cade," she panted, fear heavy on her chest, restricting her airflow. "There's no way out."

"Has to be." Racing past her, he skidded to a stop beside the last section and, dropping down, shoved at the boxes. They didn't budge. The approaching forklift's lights bore down on them, yet his resolve didn't waver. He switched to the opposite side. This time, the boxes shifted.

Tori knelt beside him, pushing with all her might, too scared to risk a glance and measure the dwindling distance. Inch by excruciating inch, they dislodged the boxes.

"We're running out of time!" Tori yelled above the engine's rumble.

She couldn't keep from looking and trying to see past the lights to the driver. Yards were all that was left between escape and a terrible confrontation.

Cade's hands closed on either side of her waist. "Go! Crawl through to the other side!"

He didn't give her a chance to argue, pushing and prodding until she was completely in the space. Tori didn't want to think about the thousands of pounds of gear above her and what might happen if the driver decided to ram the forklift into the structure.

With a final push, the obstacles tumbled out of her way, and she shimmied through. She twisted around, expecting to see Cade right behind her. But he wasn't.

He wasn't there, and she could no longer see him.

Cade crouched near the space where Tori had crawled through, weighing his options. Various scenarios flashed through his mind. Shoot out the lights, taking away the driver's advantage? Too close. He risked getting a face full of exploding glass. Leap onto the forks and risk taking another bullet or getting rammed into the wall? Nah.

"Cade Lawrence McMann, you get over here this second!"

The anger in Tori's voice jarred him. Through the opening, he glimpsed her distraught features.

The forklift jolted to a standstill.

"I'll come and get you if I have to." She gripped the sides and prepared to reenter the shelves.

"No need, sweetheart," he grunted, doing a belly-crawl to her side, all the while forming new strategies.

She snagged his wrist and tugged, not releasing him even when he gained his feet.

"Don't do that again," she hissed.

"I'm not letting him get away."

Her hold was like an iron shackle. "And I'm not letting you get yourself killed."

Retreating footsteps resonated through the building. In silent agreement, he and Tori gave chase.

Forging ahead so that he'd bear the brunt of any surprise attacks, Cade led the way past the remaining shelves into an open space with tables for sorting used gear. A plastic bin hit the floor, and he slowed as combat helmets bounced and rolled into their path.

The scrape of a metal door against concrete and the hum of distant cars passing on the road meant he was out of the building. They were losing him.

Cade burst through the door in time to see the lanky figure scrambling down the ramp. He favored his right leg. A streetlamp glinted on his hair, a distinct shade of red.

"It is Heath," Tori exclaimed, coming up beside him. "I didn't want to believe it."

His fingers skimmed her back. "Let's follow him. He's going in the opposite direction of his truck."

Keeping their eyes glued to the young lance corporal, they took the same route to the parking lot between the buildings.

"He's heading for the main road," she said, panting, her confusion evident.

"He's lost a lot of blood." They jogged side by side. At a distant intersection, the light turned green. "Maybe he's disoriented."

As Heath neared the stop sign, he slowed slightly to peer over his shoulder. Seeing them advancing, he sprinted into the two-lane street.

Tori let out a gasp of dismay. "Watch out!"

Cade watched in disbelief as a heavy-duty pickup truck slammed on its brakes and a compact car in the oncoming lane swerved over the white line. Headlights flickered across Heath, who straddled the center yellow lines. Face frozen, he hesitated a fraction of a second too long.

The truck veered sharply to avoid the collision, but it wasn't enough.

Tori screamed as Heath was thrown to the ground.

Cade moved in front of her and pulled her against him, tucking her cheek beneath his chin. He was torn between wanting to shelter her from the grim situation and trying to help the injured Marine.

Behind them, car doors opened and slammed. People spoke in panicked voices.

She nudged him away, her gaze downcast. "Go. Help him."

"But—"

"Despite the horrible things he's done, he doesn't deserve to lie there and suffer."

He stifled the need to kiss her. "Don't wander off."

"I'm not going anywhere."

"Where's Cade? Why can't I see him?" Tori flicked an errant strand out of her eyes. "He's not in trouble, is he? Because he didn't do anything wrong."

The Marine who'd brought her into the CIF warehouse half an hour ago—a senior member of the military police—assessed her with bloodshot eyes. "As I told you before, ma'am, Staff Sergeant McMann is being interviewed in a separate location. Now, I need for you to walk me through tonight's events."

He cocked his head toward the door where they'd entered. Huge round lights affixed to the ceiling had been turned on, so bright they were giving her a headache. Or was it the need for sleep? Last time she checked, it had been past 2:00 a.m. and she was functioning on the last reserves of energy she had left.

"I've already told you everything."

She curled her hands into fists and focused on remaining calm. Actually, she was trying desperately not to relive the moment of impact between Heath and the huge truck. Cade had rushed in to lend aid to the lance corporal, along with the driver of the truck and a handful of onlookers. She'd waited on the sidelines, pacing in the night and praying for her enemy. He deserved to pay for his crimes, of course, but she couldn't help hoping he survived. She had no idea how severe his injuries were. Before she could reunite with Cade, the MPs had arrived on the scene and, acting on a bystander's tip, descended on her.

While the Marine's face was a blank slate, his mouth communicated displeasure. Because he was working the night shift? Because he didn't believe her account of events? "We want to be certain none of the details were left out, ma'am."

Near the desk and an enclosed space surrounded with metal fencing, three more Marines huddled in a cluster, shooting her frequent glances. Whether intentional or not, they made her feel like a criminal. It made her worry how they were treating one of their own.

She straightened her aching shoulders. "And once I'm done, you'll take me to Cade?"

Without answering, he motioned to the shelving units, his pad of paper and pen clenched in his palm.

Praying for a gracious spirit when what she really wanted was to rail at him, Tori once again relayed the events that culminated with Heath's accident. She would've asked him if he had an update on Heath's condition if she thought he'd answer her.

Her throat was parched and her feet numb by the time he escorted her to a waiting base police car. The scene where the accident had occurred was roped off with yellow tape.

"Where are we going?"

"Provost Marshal's Office."

Tori didn't speak as he opened the front passenger door for her. Why bother? At least he hadn't forced her into the back.

Neither spoke during the short ride. At the older brick building, she was escorted through the rear entrance and along a nondescript hall flanked by rooms with tinted doors. Her relentless interrogator halted before one and reached for the knob.

She hung back. "Am I under arrest?"

"Not that I'm aware of, ma'am."

He pushed the door wide enough for her to see inside. Her gaze collided with a familiar, beloved face. Cade shoved out of his chair, relief churning in his blue eyes. She entered the room, barely aware of the door closing. They were finally alone.

She wasn't sure who moved first. The instant his arms closed around her, hugging her tightly, Tori's body went limp with relief. He was strong. Immovable. Implacable.

She let herself lean on him and refused to feel guilty about it.

Snaking her hands up his taut flanks, she pressed her cheek to the spot where his heart thundered behind sleek muscle and sinew. "You're okay."

He caressed her back. "I'm fine." Tilting her chin up, he searched her face with a grave gaze. "They treated you with respect, did they not? Because if anyone crossed the line—"

"I had to repeat my story numerous times. That's my only complaint." She frowned. "That's not true. They wouldn't tell me where you were or what was happening. You aren't going to be demoted or anything, are you?"

He shook his head. "Nothing like that."

Tori couldn't be sure what inspired the emotions swelling in her heart—the fatigue making her light-headed, the aftermath of fighting for her life or the look in Cade's eyes that reminded her of their one, magical summer together.

Don't be naive, her heart warned. *You can't trust your feelings, not when life has been reduced to hour-by-hour survival. Look where loving Cade got you last time. Heartbroken and alone.*

"Tori…" He cupped her cheek, his gaze dropping to her mouth.

Self-preservation told her to stop this before it started.

The door opened behind her, taking the decision out of her hands. She eased out of his embrace.

"You're both free to go." An older Marine waved them into the hall. "Staff Sergeant, your chain of command will follow up with you in the coming days."

"I understand, sir."

They were driven to the warehouse to retrieve her

brother's car. Cade held out his hand for the keys, which she gladly relinquished.

Her gaze was drawn to the roped-off area and remaining MPs. "How bad was it, Cade?"

His brow furrowed. "He was unconscious. The only visible injury was a gash on his head. And of course, the knife wound."

"The EMTs didn't give you any information?"

"No." He caught sight of her phone. "Who are you calling?"

"Jason. He needs to know." She didn't relish telling him their suspicions had been confirmed. "I have no idea how he'll handle the news."

"I suggest you wait until we have more details. We know Heath's involved, but not what role he plays." He stroked his jaw, where a shadow of a beard darkened his skin. "His behavior baffles me. He bolted in the woods, abandoning Aaron before deciding to double back. At the condo, he had you in a vulnerable position, but again, he left the scene. My gut tells me he's not a willing participant in this game."

"He's a good Marine, isn't he?"

Still observing the crash site, he jerked a nod. "I've watched him mature over the past year. He's gained confidence in his abilities and begun to mentor younger guys. Such a waste."

"We will get answers."

His lips turned down. "Won't change the fact that he's ruined his career and his life." Catching sight of her wide yawn, he opened her door and waited until she was settled in the plush seat before going around to the driver's side.

Tori slipped her phone in her pocket and rested her head against the headrest. Exhaustion seeped into her limbs, and she had trouble keeping her eyes open. When he turned onto the road that led to the back gate instead of the main one and the city of Jacksonville, she turned toward him.

"I thought we were going to the hospital."

"We're both beat."

"You're trained to function on little sleep, so I'm guessing you're more concerned about my civilian sensibilities."

"Neither of us will be able to function if we don't get a few hours of rest, at least." He glanced her way. "We'll go to my house. It's closer, not to mention secure. Aaron knows that if he tries to breach the system, there'll be a swift response from the authorities."

"What about Heath?"

"I contacted Claxton. He's sending Deputy Avery to stand guard."

"Stand guard?" Suddenly alert, she studied his profile. "You think he's in danger?"

"Does Aaron strike you as the kind of person who'd tolerate loose ends?"

They were hoping to pry information from Heath if—no, *when*—he regained consciousness. Aaron was smart enough to know that and cruel enough to silence his own partner-in-crime.

Tori stared out the window at the passing lights, praying the end of this nightmare was near.

SIXTEEN

Cade parked inside his garage and, leaving Tori in the car, did a quick sweep of the house. She trudged into the kitchen and leaned against the center island. She had the dazed look of someone who'd been through a firefight and was having troubling processing all that she'd witnessed.

His chest tight with tenderness, he guided her to the couch and nudged her onto the cushions. "I'll bring you something cold to drink."

She sat without speaking, her eyes big and dark, green seas of introspection.

He left her long enough to gather a couple of cans of non-caffeinated soda, strawberry yogurts and string cheese. "I brought you a snack, in case you're hungry."

After depositing everything on the coffee table, he opened the soda can and handed her the fizzing drink. She accepted it with a tired sigh.

"Thank you, Cade."

He got comfortable with his own drink, unable to look away. "Want to talk about it?"

Her pale brows collided. "About what, exactly?"

"Anything. Everything. This week you've experienced

more violence and endured more stress than the average person does in a lifetime. It can be a lot to process."

Tori took another long drink and then fiddled with the metal tab. "I wouldn't know where to start. Besides, I don't think I'm capable of stringing rational thoughts together at the moment."

"Of course. You need rest, not deep conversations."

Her gaze lifted to his face. "I will want to talk about it, eventually."

"I'll be here."

A quizzical look entered her eyes. "How do you do it?"

"Do what?"

"Make everything look easy. You don't falter. Don't crumble. You meet every obstacle with unwavering fortitude." She wagged her finger. "And don't say it's your training. It's more than that."

"You're right. Training only takes you so far." Leaning forward, he set his can on the table. "The older I get, I see how imperative it is that I fully rely on God. He's my strength and my guide."

"I admire your faith. I have to admit, I've allowed my relationship with the Lord to slip in my priorities. I got busy, you know? Distracted. First by what happened with Patrick, then the move. These past days have shown me how desperately I need Him." She ran her hand over her face, weariness in the gesture. "No one can give me peace like He can. No one else can calm the storm inside."

Needing to comfort her, Cade shifted on the cushions and settled his arm around her shoulders. "We all get distracted sometimes. We just have to right our course every once in a while."

"I'm glad He's a kind and forgiving Father."

"Me, too." He watched her twisting that ring round

and round. With his free hand, he touched the silver dolphin. "What's up with the ring?"

Her fingers stilled. "You don't remember?"

"Should I?"

"You and I went to the county fair the summer before senior year." Nostalgia softened her features. "We rode the Ferris wheel and ate caramel popcorn and corn dogs. You played a dozen games, trying to win me a stuffed animal, and when you failed to do so, you dragged me to the arts-and-crafts pavilion and ordered me to pick out something."

He lifted her hand to inspect the ring more closely. "I remember now. You and I were just friends at that point, but I couldn't keep my eyes off you. I seized every opportunity to impress you."

"If memory serves, you spent almost fifty dollars at the ring-toss booth. You were angry, but tried to hide it." Her soft chuckle washed over him like air-conditioning on a sweltering day.

"I would've spent a thousand if it meant getting you to see me as more than a friend."

Her smile faded, and she inched to the cushion's edge, forcing him to remove his arm. She rose to her feet.

"Thanks for the drink. I'm going to head upstairs."

Cade remained seated.

"Why do you still wear it?"

Tori stopped at the bottom of the steps. Turning back, regret pulsed in the green depths. "As a reminder of happier times, I guess."

Cade wanted to believe the gesture had deeper meaning—a sign that she held on to hope that one day they'd have a second chance. He shut down those thoughts. Tori hadn't indicated anything of the sort, even after their kiss at the condo. He had no idea what she wanted from him. Maybe she was merely tolerating his presence, biding her time until she no longer needed protection. It was entirely possible she would order him out of her life.

"Good night, Cade."

"Good night."

He sat there for a long time after her retreat. The house was silent, save for the ticking of an ornate clock.

Once, he'd been convinced of her love and affection. That moment when he'd gotten on one knee, and she'd gotten teary-eyed and flustered and stammered out a hearty *yes*, he'd rested in the assurance that she was to be his wife. For always.

The memory molded his heart into a tender, bruised mass.

He didn't know what was happening between them. Or maybe he did, but he wasn't willing to examine it too closely. He'd loved this woman once before and been burned. Devastated to the point he'd avoided close relationships in the decade since.

Loving and losing Tori again wouldn't damage him. It would destroy him.

Watching Heath sleep the next morning, Tori didn't notice her brother's approach until he was right next to her.

"Jason." She shifted to block his view of the hospital bed. "You didn't have to come," she said softly.

His bleak gaze examined her person, no doubt searching for new injuries Heath might've wrought. She self-consciously touched her neck. This morning, after a scant few hours of sleep and a quick, bracing shower, she'd taken stock of her appearance and hadn't liked what she'd seen. Her cheek was pink and swollen, and the bruises on her neck had taken on an ugly yellowish-purple hue. At least she was clean and wearing her own clothes, for a change.

"Has he regained consciousness?"

"No." Since Cade was Heath's platoon leader, the doctor had shared information with him. "Because of his prolonged unconscious state, they performed a CT scan and discovered a minor brain bleed. He's been placed in a medically induced coma to allow his body time to heal."

Jason circumvented her, solemnly taking in the curtained-off area where Heath was hooked up to a breathing machine and multiple IVs. A bandage covered the head wound. Dried blood streaked the skin around his ear. His freckles stood out against his milk-white skin.

When he didn't speak, she said, "They're going to monitor him for a few days and decide when to wean him off the medications."

Anger rippled in the air around him. Fisting his hands at his sides, he said through clenched teeth, "I plan to be here when they do. I want to be the first to question him."

Tori stepped closer and squeezed his shoulder. "You couldn't have known, so stop blaming yourself."

"I let him into my life. I shared private stuff." His head dipped. "Stuff about you."

"I know we've had our hiccups lately. It's natural to vent to friends."

"Except he wasn't my friend. He used me to get to you."

Tori wished she could absorb his frustration and hurt. "Jason—"

"Hey." Cade walked up with Deputy Avery, who'd asked to speak with him ten minutes prior. They'd retreated to a spot beyond the nurses' station. He looked at her and Jason. "Got a minute?"

They left the deputy to watch over Heath. So far, there'd been no one lurking around the ICU unit. Hospital security had been briefed about the possibility of Aaron Waters coming after the lance corporal. That they didn't know how many others Aaron had enlisted in his revenge scheme or their identities was a disadvantage, so they weren't taking any chances.

Cade led them to a bank of elevators, which they took to the lobby and the bustling cafeteria. Breakfast was still being served, and the salty smell of fried eggs and sausage greeted her. Jason snagged a chocolate milk and energy bar, while she and Cade poured their second cups of coffee for the day.

In a far corner booth, Cade scooted in beside Tori and studied Jason over the rim of his Styrofoam cup.

"Brett gave you a ride here?"

Twisting the lid off his milk, he shook his head. "He had to stick around the condo and wait for the insurance people. I called a work buddy to pick me up."

He hadn't been pleased that they'd waited until morning to tell him the news.

"We'll give you a ride home," Cade said.

Tori looked at him. "We're leaving?"

"Nothing we can do here. Heath can't talk to us. Even if he was awake, there's no guarantee he would offer Aaron up on a silver platter. Too many unknowns."

"The sheriff's department is looking into possible connections between them, right?"

"Deputy Avery reassured me they're pulling more guys onto the case." He shifted on the hard plastic seat. "He did have a development. Lamont and Truman have alibis for the night we were run off the road. Both deny knowing Aaron and having anything to do with the attacks on us. There's no proof to say otherwise, but the deputies will continue to dig."

Tori gazed at the faces of the strangers around them. Any one of these people could be working with Aaron— evil disguised in plain sight. Foreboding skittered up her spine. After the upheaval of recent days, she craved peace and calm.

"Jason," Cade began, "Deputy Avery wants you to speak with him or Claxton when you're feeling up to it."

His blue eyes arrested and he gulped down a bite of energy bar. "Me? Why?"

"To discuss your association with Heath. You're not in trouble. They're simply hoping to gain information. Details you might think are irrelevant but they could use to connect pieces of the puzzle."

His gaze downcast, he nodded. "I'll go today."

Cade and Tori exchanged a glance.

"You're not the first to be deceived by someone," Cade said. "I imagine it doesn't feel good to learn you've been lied to, but you've got to put it behind you."

He crumpled the empty wrapper into a ball. "You would've seen through his act."

"He's in my platoon. If anyone should've picked up on Heath's secret activities, it's me."

Tori leaned across the table and laid her hand on Jason's. "I've been where you are. I've experienced the shame and self-doubts. You and Heath were buddies for a brief time. I *dated* a fraud." At his quick, upward glance, she said, "I wasted a portion of my life in a relationship with someone capable of major crimes."

"Patrick."

"It's not something I'm proud of. I still question my judgment sometimes. But I've also realized that I'm not responsible for his actions. Just as you aren't responsible for Heath's."

The glimpse of pain in her brother's eyes punched her in the gut. "You could've died, sis. And it would've been my fault."

Tears welled. Uncaring about the lack of privacy, Tori switched to his side of the booth and wrapped her arms around him. "I'm alive because God's not finished with me yet. There's a verse that says our days are accounted for before we're even born. I've got more days to live, Jase."

A shudder rippled through him. "I'm sorry."

Tori hugged him tighter and then released him. Words and reassurances would only go so far. Jason would have to work through this on his own terms. "Cade and I will come with you to the sheriff's office. We'll sit with you during the interview, if you want."

"I'll go alone." His mouth twisted. "You and Cade could be mistaken for extras on the latest zombie flick. Go home before you start scaring small children."

Cade chuckled. Tori recognized the humor as an attempt to deflect from the emotionally charged moment. She hated that Jason had been put in this position and vowed to support him in whatever capacity he'd allow.

A security guard accompanied them to the parking lot. Stepping outside the hospital felt like leaving a blast chiller and entering a sauna. Anxiety crawled across her skin like tiny spiders. What did all those car windows conceal? The pines and shrubs surrounding the lot provided ample hiding places.

She never used to fear public spaces. Quite the opposite. Tori reveled spending time outside, whether it be riding her bike at the park, renting kayaks at the lake or swimming in the ocean.

Thanks to one sick, twisted man, her and Cade's lives had been altered, their freedom restricted to hiding behind walls and windows.

As they approached the car, Cade touched her arm. "This isn't a life sentence," he murmured. "Soon you'll be free to go and do as you please."

Tori glanced at him in surprise. How was it possible he still knew her well enough to guess her thoughts?

His eyes darkened. "And you won't be forced to spend your days with your ex-fiancé."

When he'd shown up on her doorstep, she'd wanted him—and the difficult, confusing feelings he stirred up—gone. Now the prospect of *not* seeing him, except for the occasional glimpse across town, hurt. Hurt badly. Left her hollow inside and slightly panicked.

The chasm that time and distance had wrought was growing smaller by the day and past wounds eclipsed by the reforging of the friendship that had made what they'd shared so special. Cade had saved her life. He'd protected and comforted her. He'd become the person she turned to for reassurance. He'd become her rock, just like he'd been all those years ago. And that frightened her almost as much as another encounter with Aaron.

Tori couldn't be falling for him all over again. Could she?

SEVENTEEN

"I wish we could've gone to church."

Tori had positioned herself at the window with a street view of Cade's neighborhood. They'd agreed to keep the blinds closed. Although his home was beautiful and cozy, it was too much like a cave, the sunlight peeking around the edges taunting her.

She peeled the slats apart. Across the street, an elderly couple dressed in their Sunday best and Bible in hand got out of their rusty Oldsmobile and meandered to the house. Ridiculous that she experienced a pang of jealousy. But it seemed ages since she'd been able to worship with her fellow believers and listen to her pastor's sermons. Attending church wasn't a chore for Tori. It was an uplifting experience, a time of refreshing and encouragement.

Cade tossed the magazine he'd been perusing to the coffee table. He rose and stretched. The soft cotton of his Marine-green T-shirt mapped his broad chest and muscular arms. She wanted those strong arms to be hugging her…

Cheeks heating, she prayed he didn't guess the direction of her thoughts. Being sequestered alone together was hard enough without having to deal with the attraction that lurked beneath the surface.

"I know what you mean," he said. "If this were a normal Sunday, I'd be on the patio, grilling steaks and potatoes right after services."

Tori made an appreciative noise. "With a garden salad and fresh-baked rolls?"

A laugh gusted out of him. "Salad in a bag and frozen rolls are the best I can manage."

"Sounds wonderful." It didn't take much for her to envision a lazy afternoon spent in his company. A relaxed afternoon free of the worries that accompanied being targeted for murder.

His regard turned compassionate. Was he reading her mind again? Assessing her moods with his astute gaze?

Letting the blinds fall into place, she said, "Julian is supposed to bring groceries this afternoon?"

She hoped Julian would stick around for a while, if only to give her a reprieve from the feelings Cade inspired.

"The basics." He nodded. "For lunch, we'll have to make do with sandwiches."

"Bologna and cheese on white triangles?" she said, referring to their moms' go-to picnic choices when she and Cade were younger.

He grinned. "These will be a little more sophisticated than that."

Her phone buzzed. "Cade, I don't recognize this number."

Dark brows crashing together, he came to stand beside her. "Put it on speaker."

On edge, Tori answered the call.

"Tori?"

The feminine voice sounded familiar, but she couldn't pinpoint it.

"Yes?"

"This is Felicia Ortiz. I'm here at the store with your mom—"

Her heart leaped. "Has something happened? Is she okay?"

"We were doing some light cleaning when she had an episode." Another voice sounded in the background. "She's insisting that she's fine."

Cade's hand came to rest low on her back, a steady anchor point to keep her from flying apart.

"What kind of episode?"

"Short of breath. Weak. Dizzy." Felicia's voice was calm and matter-of-fact. "But she doesn't have any other symptoms that might indicate an emergency issue. I simply thought you should know. I've tried to convince her to go home, or at least go upstairs to your apartment and rest for a while."

"But she's not listening," Tori surmised, shooting an exasperated glance at Cade, whose eyes bore evidence of his own concern. "I'm coming over there."

"Maybe she'll listen to you."

"Thanks for calling, Felicia." The conversation ended and she shifted away from Cade. "Don't try to talk me out of going. I'll go by myself if I have to. Call a taxi or—"

He tipped her chin up. "I want to check on her, too. We'll go together."

Relief tangled up with gratitude. "Thank you for understanding."

Cade fired off a text to Julian, explaining where they'd be, and then ushered her to the garage. They made good time to the shop, though to Tori it felt like an eternity. She didn't even get to appreciate the beautiful summer day.

Felicia met them at the door. Tori tried and failed to get a read on her thoughts. The Marine was one cool cucumber, a good trait to have when dealing with a crisis.

"This way."

Barbara was seated at the small table in the converted office. Her face was flushed, her hair damp at her temples. Tori crouched in front of her and took her hand.

"Mom."

"Don't use that tone with me, young lady." Patting Tori's hand, she managed a trembling smile. "I was dusting the merchandise, that's all."

Felicia, who'd taken up a spot by the fridge, cleared her throat. "You were climbing up and down the ladder to reach the light fixtures and picture frames."

"In this heat?" Tori said. "Leave those tasks for me, okay?"

"You shouldn't have brought her," Barbara told Cade. "I'm fine."

He held up his palms. "I couldn't have reasoned with her if I'd tried."

"She listens to you more than you think, Cade."

"Mom," Tori said again.

The bell jangled in the front of the house, signaling a customer. Felicia went to greet them. Barbara sipped on her bottled water and peppered them with questions about the case. As promised, Jason had gone to the sheriff's department yesterday. To their knowledge, there hadn't been any new developments.

Her mother's color crept back into the normal range. With the topic of their pursuers exhausted, she said, "Cade, can you give us a minute alone?"

"Of course."

He joined Felicia and the customer in the front room. Their muted conversation whispered through the open spaces.

Tori straightened and took the seat opposite. "What's on your mind?"

"I haven't had a minute alone with you since this ordeal began. How are you coping with everything?"

"Mom, I didn't come here to discuss my frame of mind. I'm worried about you. You should call your doctor's answering service. Or at the very least, go to a walk-in clinic."

"I got overheated, that's all." She waved away her concerns. "You've been thrown together with Cade, which goes against your initial plan of burying your head in the sand and pretending he doesn't exist. Has anything changed between you two?"

"Being home has brought up a lot of old memories and emotions."

She clapped her hands together. "I knew it. You and Cade were meant for each other—"

"I'm not talking about Cade, Mom. I'm talking about Dad."

Her lips parted. "What brought this on?"

Tori understood her reaction. She'd resisted this discussion since the day Marines knocked on their door with the news that Thomas James had been killed in action.

"I've been forced to take a closer look at myself, and I'm not sure I like what I see. I'm to blame for our fractious relationship, aren't I?"

She sobered. "Tori, your father was an outstanding Marine. Unfortunately, he didn't have a clue how to be a family man. He loved you and delighted in you. But as you got older, he couldn't figure out how to communicate. He was more afraid of a teenage girl and her roller-coaster emotions than he was of enemy fire."

"I made things harder on him than they needed to be, though. I couldn't see that then, but as an adult looking back…" She clenched her fists, unexpected grief slamming into her. "I have regrets. A host of them."

Barbara cupped her cheek, love shining in her eyes. "Don't be so hard on yourself. You were a young girl who needed her father to be there for her. You dealt with your disappointment in your own way."

"Sometimes I think that if I hadn't been so needy and demanding, he would've come around more often."

"No. That was my doing." Lowering her hand to her lap, she shook her head sadly. "I should've told you a long time ago, but not all of his absences can be blamed on his job. Sometimes, when he and I were fighting, I asked him to stay at the base hotel."

Tori bowed her head, grappling with the revelation. He'd stayed away out of consideration for her mom? She wanted to be angry, but she hadn't walked in her mom's shoes, hadn't been inside their relationship. Sorrow over lost chances filled her.

"Please forgive me, Tori. I didn't take into account the effect my decisions would have on you."

Wiping away a rogue tear, Tori hugged her. "I love you, Mom."

Barbara hugged her as if she'd never let go. "Are we okay?"

"We're okay, as long as you promise not to climb any more ladders in the near future."

Cade met Julian at the door. "Did you get what I asked for?"

Clutching bags in each hand, he lifted one an inch. "I had to get one for myself. Couldn't resist."

Relieving him of the grocery bags, Cade followed him through the living room and into the kitchen.

"I'll take mine with me." Julian flashed a sly grin. "Wouldn't want to intrude on your romantic meal."

Cade glanced over his shoulder, relieved Tori was upstairs and couldn't have overheard. "You've got the wrong idea. In fact, Tori would probably prefer it if you did stick around for a while."

Stacking the three plastic containers on the counter, he arched a brow. "You getting on each other's nerves already?"

"That's not it."

The edginess he'd sensed in her yesterday and today had become amplified since their return from the shop. It went deeper than the threat against them. Deeper than worry about her mom. If he had to guess, he'd say *he* was the problem. They'd been growing closer, and she'd hit the brakes. Thrown up an invisible wall.

He wouldn't lie. It hurt. But her comfort and well-being were his priority, and he was determined to make this waiting game as bearable as possible. If that meant passing the days in separate areas of the house or asking Julian to bring steaks every night, so be it.

Crossing his arms, Julian watched as Cade unpacked the items.

"This situation would be difficult for anyone," he said. "Add your history into the mix, and it becomes even more complicated."

Cade shuffled cartons of milk and juice around on the shelf. Complicated? That was one way of putting it.

"Oh. Hi, Tori."

At Julian's soft greeting, Cade closed the fridge. She hovered in the arched opening, pretty in a sleeveless blue dress with raised white stitching along the knee-length hem. Below that, her legs were smooth and pale. He remembered that she used to complain about her fair complexion and the need to constantly pile on sunscreen. Round-toed flats completed the look.

Her smile was directed at Julian. "Something smells delicious. What did you find at the grocery store?"

Motioning her over, he flipped the lid on the top container. "Not grocery store. Cade sent me on a mission to find the best steaks in Sneads Ferry."

Tori took an appreciative sniff. "If they taste as good as they look, we're in for a treat. You're going to stay, aren't you?"

Over her head, Cade shot Julian an I-told-you-so look. Not missing a beat, Julian grinned.

"Of course."

While Cade gathered utensils and poured chilled tea into glasses, Julian and Tori transferred the food to plates. They gathered around the breakfast table and, after a brief prayer of thanks, dug into the meal. He didn't offer much in the way of conversation. Instead, he was content to listen as Tori peppered Julian first with questions about his childhood in Hawaii, and then about his career as a Special Forces Marine. His accounts were limited to humorous mishaps involving his fellow Marines and interesting aspects of his initial training. The crowd-friendly version of his job.

When they'd eaten their fill, Tori surprised Cade with a light touch on his hand. "Thank you for the meal, Cade. It was wonderful."

"I couldn't grill them myself. This was the next best option." He waved his fork at Julian. "Besides, all I did was give him the list. He's the one who picked up everything."

"I'm just glad you didn't forget about dessert," Julian piped up. After carrying his plate to the sink, he pulled a pink-and-white box from the fridge. "*Crème horns* anyone?"

Tori's gaze centered on Cade. "You remembered?"

"Fresh from your favorite bakery."

Her quick smile lifted his spirits. "Chocolate or vanilla filling?"

"Some of each."

When Julian placed the box in the middle of the round table, Tori didn't waste any time claiming one of the spiral pastries. At her groan of pleasure, Julian laughed and gave him a thumbs-up.

"No one else makes *crème horns* like this," she enthused.

Without thinking, Cade reached over and swept the powdered sugar off her upper lip with his thumb. She stilled, her lips parting and eyes deepening to pine-needle green. Was she remembering their kiss?

He stood abruptly, stacked her plate atop his and busied himself loading the dishwasher. *Remember your goal, McMann. Make her comfortable. She needs you to be her friend, not the man who used to love her.*

Used to?

Cade's heart slowed. Sweat beaded his upper lip. A glass slipped from his fingers and crashed to the floor, splintering into jagged pieces.

Tori gathered the broom and the dustpan. "You didn't cut yourself, did you?"

"No. Just lost my grip." Taking them from her, he suggested she and Julian choose a movie they could all watch.

When they'd gone into the living room, he stood without moving, crushing the broom handle in his grip.

Somewhere along the way, the line between past and present had disappeared. He'd assumed his feelings for Tori had been neatly filed away under the file of immature youth experience. A hard lesson learned—real-life romance wasn't like the sappy movies Tori had convinced him to watch with her.

He'd made a tactical error.

He'd fallen in love with Victoria James a second time. Not the shy, sweet girl she'd been at eighteen. The strong, independent, unshakable woman she'd become.

And once again, he was going to suffer for it.

EIGHTEEN

Something was bothering Cade.

Lounging on the far end of the couch, his smiles at the movie's jokes were perfunctory at best. There was an odd tension in him, a grimness in his posture that filled her with cold foreboding. Tori had been glad for Julian's presence during supper because it helped distract her from the swirling attraction between Cade and herself. Now she was counting down the minutes until she could question him alone.

What exactly had put that fearsome intensity in his eyes?

Could he have received a text from Deputy Claxton? Bad news he was reluctant to share with her?

Tori felt his gaze light on her, more specifically her bobbing foot.

"Nervous about something?" he murmured.

She forced herself to still. "Nothing in particular."

Looking over at the armchair Julian had claimed, she noticed him typing into his phone, brows snapped together in concentration.

"Sorry, guys." He rose and pocketed the device. "I have to go. Duty calls."

Cade paused the film. "More training?"

"If you don't hear from me in the next few days, you'll know it's the real deal."

The glint in his eyes reminded Tori of her dad. He'd had that same expression right before a mission—a puzzling mix of resignation and anticipation. Although she didn't know the Special Forces Marine that well, she liked him because he was Cade's friend and he'd helped her, a stranger, with no expectation of anything in return. She didn't like to think of him in harm's way.

"You're in my prayers, Julian," she told him.

Surprise lit his dark eyes. "Thanks, Tori."

Cade slapped him on the back. "Mine, too, brother."

When he'd gone, Cade rearmed the system and turned to her. "I'm not in the mood to finish the movie. Do you mind watching the rest without me?"

"What are you going to do?"

"I'll be in my office for a while." He indicated a door opposite the guest bathroom. "My laptop's in there."

"What's on your mind, Cade? Have you heard something about the case that you're afraid to tell me?"

His eyes widened. "No, I wouldn't keep information like that from you."

"Have I done something?"

"No." His gaze cut away, and he kneaded the back of his neck. "You've been the perfect houseguest."

"But you're eager to return to your life," she surmised. He'd never hurt her by saying so, though. "I understand. You've lived the bachelor's lifestyle for years, and now you're saddled with me twenty-four-seven."

He swallowed hard. "Tori, I…"

"You can tell me. I won't break."

When his gaze met hers, a storm churned in the blue depths. "I guess you're right. I'm used to having time to myself."

Tori fought to keep her expression schooled. After all, she'd asked for the truth, hadn't she? "I'm praying this ends soon."

He grimaced. "We'll both be able to resume our normal routines."

She jerked her thumb over her shoulder. "I'm going to take a bath and go to bed."

"Good night, Tori."

"Good night."

She climbed the stairs with leaden feet. Being an unwanted burden was the worst feeling.

That wasn't true. The worst was knowing Cade had stuck by her side out of a sense of duty, and his patience was wearing thin.

After a long bath, Tori dressed in her soft pants and a T-shirt and entered the bedroom. Quiet blanketed the house. Spying her phone and earbuds on the pillow, she crossed to the bed. Music usually lulled her to sleep. Hopefully it would do the trick tonight and soothe her troubled spirit. Stretching across the wide bed, she was reaching for the phone when she happened to glance up.

There, in the mirror opposite, was the reflection of the man who haunted her days and nights.

Before she could react, Aaron was upon her, pinning her arms to prevent her from striking out.

She screamed for Cade.

Aaron's gloved hand came down on her mouth, crushing her lips against her teeth. His grin was sickly triumphant. "Your boyfriend won't be coming to your rescue this time."

Battling the numbing effects of sheer terror, Tori struggled to get free. What had he done with Cade? Why hadn't the alarm triggered?

The sudden sharp sting in her neck came as a terrible shock. Shoving her to the bed, he loomed over her, brandishing a needle and syringe. "You'll soon find, Tori, that you don't have enough strength to walk on your own. Weakness will set in, and I'll carry you out to my car. You won't have the strength to fight me or attempt to escape."

Tori scrambled to the far edge. Already, her limbs didn't want to cooperate. "What did you do to Cade?"

"I didn't drug him. Didn't have to. I knocked him out and trussed him up like a prize steer." Placing the syringe on the bedside table, he stalked around the bed and, producing a strip of cloth from his pocket, attempted to gag her.

Tori shifted and did her best to avoid his hands. She was growing woozy, her movements uncoordinated. He gripped her chin in a punishing hold. "It's useless to resist, you know." He ran his fingers across her temple, past her ear and under her chin. "So beautiful. A pity you have to die, but I have my orders."

Moaning, Tori closed her eyes and shook her head. This couldn't be happening.

Cade, where are you?

Aaron got the gag in place. Drained of her energy, he maneuvered her into a sitting position and tied it off. Tears of frustration pricked her eyelids. She was like a limp rag doll as he thrust the covers aside and lifted her into his arms.

"We're going for a ride, Tori." His gray eyes glittered with menacing promise. "Don't worry, you'll be asleep for most of it."

Tori angled her head away from his chest, her bleary gaze searching for Cade as they descended the stairs and entered the dim living room. A garbled sound startled her. Aaron stopped. Shone the flashlight onto the figure laid out on the couch, wrists and ankles bound with thick rope, mouth gagged like hers.

Cade.

When his burning gaze collided with hers, a warning rumbled through his chest. He struggled to free himself. Relief that he was alive seized her, followed by the terrible knowledge that this was likely the last time she'd see him.

With the unknown drug in her system, she didn't have the strength to fight her captor. And Cade wasn't going to be able to follow them.

Aaron's chuckle scraped over her raw nerves. "Take a long look, McMann. You won't be in the same room with her again." Approaching the couch, he shined the beam on the coffee table. "Keep that phone handy. You'll be receiving a video from us later today. One last message from your beloved."

Cade's struggles intensified as Aaron strode from the room. Tori couldn't stop the tears from falling as she was placed on the back seat of a car, forced to lie on her side, her view restricted by the seats. As the car lurched into motion, her lids became heavier, her thoughts increasingly disjointed.

The one truth she clung to was also her greatest regret. Cade would never know that her love for him had never died.

The edges of his vision dimmed as the engine's purr faded away, and he was left with ominous silence and the knowledge that Tori was at the mercy of a killer. The absolute terror in her wide green eyes strangled him. Her initial scream from her bedroom echoed in his ears.

Panic threatened.

He choked down the destructive emotions trying to paralyze him. He'd be no good to her if he lost it.

He tried to think of a tool he could use to cut these ropes. After Aaron had ambushed him as he'd left his study, he'd divested him of the knife he kept in his pocket. His mind empty of a solution, he tugged and twisted his hands, ignoring the discomfort of his already tender wrists. He tried to sit but tumbled to the floor instead, bumping his head against the coffee table on the way down.

That's it! The coffee table was made of wood, with an insert of thin glass. If he could break it…

Squirming onto his knees, he brought his bound hands down on the glass. Over and over. Desperation rattled through his chest and escaped in a muffled roar. He hit it again, pain registering through the haze as the glass splintered into a thousand pieces.

He located a jagged piece jutting from the corner and worked to cut the ropes. Although aware he was cutting himself in the process, he continued at a feverish pace. Minutes passed. Sweat dripped from his forehead.

And then, suddenly, he was free.

He yanked the gag off, seized the phone and dialed 911. Once he'd explained the emergency, he demanded to be connected to Claxton or Avery. He got Avery.

"You have to convince the doctors to wean Heath out of that coma," he said.

"Whoa, slow down. What's happened?"

"Are you at the hospital?" He tried to loosen the ropes around his ankles.

"Yes, why?"

"Aaron bypassed my security system. He's got Tori," he said, panting. He dragged himself across the floor to the kitchen, pulled himself up at the sink and located a knife.

"Are you hurt?"

"I'm fine. Listen, our only hope of finding Tori is to wake Heath and get him to tell us who else is working with him. He has to know where they were planning on taking her."

"Cade," he began heavily.

"Don't you dare tell me it's not doable."

"Even if they agreed, which I doubt they would, there's no guarantee he'd tell us what we need to know."

Cade bent and sliced the ropes. Flicked on a light. Splatters of blood formed a trail on the tile. His hands were slick with it. At least it was his, not Tori's.

"I'm coming there."

Before Avery could protest, Cade ended the call, grabbed the sedan's keys and tore out of the garage the second the door cleared the car's roof.

He couldn't get their last conversation out of his head. His stupid, *stupid* decision to let her assume she was nothing more than an obligation, one he was growing tired of.

Cade slammed the wheel with his fist, a shaft of discomfort traveling up his arm.

Instead of protecting her, he'd protected himself from further hurt.

And now the woman he loved more than life itself was in the enemy's hands.

NINETEEN

Aaron lied. Tori didn't fall asleep. She spent the car ride—characterized by stops and starts, curves and a series of baffling turns—battling nausea and imagining what horror was to befall her.

Where are you, Lord? Have You abandoned me? I know I'm not supposed to rely on feelings. I'm supposed to rely on Your holy Word and the promise You won't ever leave me or forsake me. Help me to remember that.

"Hey."

Aaron's voice pulled her from her thoughts.

"I'm ten minutes out." Silence. Then a sadistic chuckle. "Yeah, the system was a piece of cake to override. McMann didn't know what hit him. You should've seen his reaction when I carted her out of there."

Tori squeezed her eyes shut, reliving those final moments. If only she'd realized in time that he was the only man for her, that Cade was not only her best friend…he was her perfect match. The man she wanted by her side for always. She'd thrown it away at eighteen, too naive, too blind to see that his love was a priceless gift.

"You have the belt ready?"

Belt? What was he talking about?

Who was he talking to?

Soon, the mastermind behind these attacks would be unmasked and his ultimate goal revealed. Tori braced herself to meet the person whose hatred of Cade had spawned insanity.

Cade ignored the gasps and wary glances he received as he burst out of the stairwell on Heath's floor and stormed past the elevators and rooms. A nurse at the nurses' station spotted him and, taking in the state of his clothes and hands, bloody from the myriad of cuts, moved into his path.

"Sir, can I help you?"

"No."

At the end of the hall, Deputy Avery's eyes rounded. When Cade sidestepped the nurse and continued toward Heath's room, Avery told her he'd handle it.

"You look like you could use medical attention," he said, blocking the entrance.

"Is he awake? Did you talk to the doctors?"

"What happened to your hands, Cade?"

"Minor cuts. They can wait." His heart thundered in his chest. "Tori's running out of time. We have to talk to Heath."

He was their only hope of finding her before Aaron and his cohorts made good on their threats.

Avery shifted his stance, his hand resting on his firearm. "His doctor said it's too early to wean him off the meds."

Desperation threatened to override logic. Glaring, he crowded the shorter man. "Are you telling me that this guy's life, this guy who *attacked* Tori and tried to strangle her to death, is worth more than hers?"

"You know that's not how this works," Avery said. "I'm as concerned about her as you are—"

"Doubt it."

"You need to get yourself under control," he warned. "Otherwise, you'll be cooling your heels in lockup, and then how will you help her?"

"You don't understand—"

His phone vibrated, and his mouth went dry. He fished his phone from his pocket and his body lost some of its tension when he recognized Brett's number. He'd thought it was the video Aaron had promised. What kind of video, Cade couldn't bring himself to think about.

"I can't talk now," he told his friend.

"Wait! What's wrong?"

He ground his back teeth. Turning slightly away from the deputy, he stared at the faded painting on the wall. "Tori's been taken."

"By who? The retired Marine?"

"Yeah."

"What's he look like again?"

Bile coated his throat. "Blond. Gray eyes. Built. Tattoos."

Brett's breathing changed rhythm. "Cade, I think I know who he's working with."

He stiffened. "What? How?"

"Dante, Heath's roommate, brought me a packet of photographs last night when he reported for our night-fire exercise. He found them beneath Heath's bed. I didn't have a chance to go through them until now."

"And?"

"I found several photos—some old, some more recent—with the same four people. William Poole, Heath Polanski, a man who matches Aaron Waters's description and a brunette female."

"Do you recognize her?"

"As a matter of fact, I do. She's in intelligence. She

was with us in Afghanistan. I don't know her name. But Cade, she's got to be your mystery perpetrator. It's clear she and William were a couple."

Hope ignited. This was the clue they'd been searching for. A member of the intelligence battalion would have the knowledge and skills to rig the bomb that took out Tori's car. They'd also be adept at using long-range rifles. Sensing Avery's intense scrutiny, Cade told Brett to text him pictures.

When the first one came through, Cade had to put a hand against the wall to steady himself. "This can't be her."

"You'd better fill me in," Avery stated.

Numb, he relayed everything he knew. "This woman, Felicia Ortiz, has insinuated herself into Tori's mom's life." His blood ran cold as he recalled the times she'd had access to both Barbara and Tori. "Barbara could be in danger, too."

"On it." Avery called in the threat. He also ordered a complete probe into Felicia's life. "We've got someone headed to Barbara James's residence."

Cade nodded, his mind racing. He hadn't once been suspicious of the reserved, sharp-eyed Marine sergeant. Was she that good of an actor? Or was he that inept at reading signals?

Another picture came through. William had his arm slung around Felicia, and she was leaning into his side.

Avery tapped the screen. "Is that an engagement ring?"

He enlarged the photo. "Looks like it. If they were engaged, they kept it under wraps. She outranked him. That's a big no-no."

"There's your motive. Felicia's fiancé was killed, and she blames you."

His stomach dropped to his toes. "She found out that Tori and I used to be involved."

He'd assumed Brett had shared the information. Now he decided it must've been Barbara. She was proud of her children and loved to talk about them with her customers. There was even a photo of Tori and Cade near the shop's register. When Felicia had stepped in to help her cousin, Maria, she must've made the connection. Her grief and misplaced blame led her down the path of revenge.

"This is good news," Avery said. "We'll run down every scrap of information."

"But will it be in time to save Tori?"

Constant ticking penetrated the darkness shrouding her.

A moan escaped as she came to. Her head and neck throbbed. Disoriented, she forced her eyes open, the sense of space and florescent light registering at the same time as the motor oil and grease that were heavy in the air. She must've succumbed to the drugs after all, because the last thing she remembered was Aaron's phone conversation.

"At last," a female voice sniped. Fingers gripped Tori's chin and jerked her head up. "Time to wake up and join the party."

The woman's features came into focus. *"You."*

"I played my part well, yes?" Felicia's eyes were twin pools of callous hatred. Tori had once thought her beautiful. Now the ugliness in her soul was printed on her face.

Fear shot through her. "My mom," she gasped. "Where is she?"

"I have no reason to harm Barbara." She dismissed the notion. "In fact, I owe her. She's the one who inspired this entire plan. She simply wouldn't stop prattling on and on about her beautiful, talented daughter and her lost chance at love. She painted a picture of you and Cade that rivaled the Hollywood classics. Barbara helped me see that the best way to repay Cade for every day I've lived without William was through you. You're the one I need to make Cade miserable. And I've finally got you." To the man beside her, she said, "Got your phone ready?"

Aaron fiddled with the device and then pointed it at Tori. "Say hello to Cade, little librarian. This is your final message to him, so make it count."

"My guess is he'll watch it a thousand times, tormented by the fact that he wasn't able to save you—his first and only love."

Tori shifted on the hard chair, struggling against the rope wound around her upper body. An unusual weight registered on her midsection. She looked down and wished she hadn't woken up. Horror rocketed through her, rendering her dizzy and weak.

A metal pipe with a battery and timer and wires was strapped to her. A bomb.

They'd blown up her car, and now they were going to make sure she succumbed to the blast this time.

"Aw, she looks scared." Felicia seized the phone and spoke into it. "William didn't have a chance to be scared. He didn't have time to think about his loved ones, the family and friends he was leaving behind. Your girl will have that chance. She's got about thirty minutes to mourn her untimely demise. You, on the other hand, will have the rest of yours to hate yourself for failing her."

"Who was William to you?" Tori ventured in a quavering voice, inwardly begging God to intervene.

"My soul mate." She snagged a locket from beneath her shirt, opened it and flashed a picture of William Poole. "Cade's ineptitude stole him away."

Tori battled to ignore the relentless ticking of the timer,

which was an ordinary wind-up kitchen timer. She struggled to remain still when her instinct was to fight the ropes and try to escape. The bomb looked homemade. Who knew if the design would hold up or go off with little provocation.

Felicia continued to stare at his photo, lost in the past. For a moment, she looked like a normal, grieving fiancée. Then bitterness and hatred reclaimed her.

She dropped the locket as if it burned her and stuck her face close to Tori's. "We had plans," she cried. "He was going to serve out the remainder of his current contract. He had eight months left. Eight!" She threw her hands up. "We were so close to getting everything we ever wanted. Did you know I was in Afghanistan when it happened?"

"On patrol?"

"On the FOB. As part of the Female Engagement Team, I was supposed to accompany the guys. Act as liaison to the local females." She tugged at her hair.

Still filming, Aaron shook his head. "You can't blame yourself, Felicia. You had no choice but to stay behind that day."

Tori was starting to piece together the puzzle. Felicia didn't blame Cade as much as she blamed herself. "Why did you?"

"She was sick," Aaron supplied, his gray gaze trailing Felicia. There was more than friendly concern there.

Were the two involved? Gauging from the sergeant's mental state, Tori doubted she would entertain thoughts of another man. Aaron…he looked as if he worshiped Felicia. Was that why he'd gone along with her plan?

"Something she ate the night before didn't agree with her."

"If I'd been there, I would've prevented a tragedy."

"Or gotten yourself killed," Aaron argued.

Felicia continued to pace for long, tense moments and then appeared to pull herself together. "What's done is done. Now it's time for payback." She jerked the phone from him and shoved it in front of Tori. "What do you want to say to your beloved Cade?"

Tori stared at the phone, afraid she might be sick.

Was she really going to die in this warehouse? A violent death that would haunt Cade and her family for years? She bit down hard on her lip to keep from crying. Cade would never accept this wasn't his fault. He'd be crushed beneath the weight of guilt.

"Better hurry up," Felicia taunted. "Your time is growing short."

He'd never know how much this time with him had meant to her. Yes, they'd been in danger, but it had brought them together like nothing else could've. The time with Cade had cemented what she'd always known—he was the love of her life. Her best friend.

She'd been a fool to allow his choice of career to drive them apart.

Father God, I can't guess Your sovereign will. But if this is how it's meant to end, I pray You'll lift Cade, my mom and Jason up. Walk beside them through the aftermath. Create joy from ashes.

"You have no idea, do you?" she said.

Felicia's frown deepened. "Idea about what?"

"Aaron's in love with you."

He stiffened. Felicia shot him a confused glance.

"Why else would he do your dirty work and be willing to risk jail for you?"

"You're not as smart as you think you are, librarian. The four of us—William, Brandon, Heath and me—were childhood friends. Grew up in the same poor West Virginia town. He's as eager for vengeance as I am. Tell her, Aaron."

His gaze dropped to the cracked cement floor. "When you and William became a thing, I accepted that you'd never look at me as anything other than a friend. But after his death, I had hope again."

She looked aghast. "There will never be another man for me."

Hurt washed over him. "I can make you smile again. I know it. Give me a chance, at least."

"You can be together," Tori said. "As friends or whatever. Just let me go. You won't face murder charges. If you let me go, I'm sure you can negotiate some sort of deal—"

"Shut up," Felicia snarled, backhanding her. Pain radiated through her cheek, and her eyes smarted.

"Let's just go," Aaron urged. "Forget what she said. Forget the video."

"No." Seizing a fistful of Tori's hair, she tugged hard. "You listen to me—"

"What was that?" Aaron trotted to the nearest window. A hiss whistled between his teeth. "They've found us!"

Releasing Tori, Felicia whirled around. "Impossible."

"I see three sheriff's department vehicles." He whipped his head toward them, his eyes pinned to Tori. He stalked across the warehouse floor and jabbed his finger at her. "Do you have a tracker on you?"

"N-no."

"Then how did they find us?" The tendons bulged in his neck, and his nostrils flared. He looked like he was contemplating killing her with his bare hands. Still, hope welled inside.

"I don't know."

"We have to go." Felicia flung her hand toward the

pair of motorcycles parked near a rear metal door. "We can escape out the back while they're casing the front."

Together, they jogged to the motorcycles and grabbed their helmets.

The ticking of the timer reminded Tori the danger hadn't passed. The authorities had no idea a bomb was involved. There wouldn't be time to call in a SWAT team to disarm it.

Sweat trickled down her spine. Fear lodged in her throat.

Had they found her too late?

Aaron was straddling his bike and Felicia was pulling on her helmet when movement registered in Tori's peripheral vision. A man entered through the same door the pair intended to use for an escape. A man in jeans and a black T-shirt with the McMann fishing logo. A man whom she'd believed she might never see again.

Her heart stuttered. Cade.

"Hold it right there," he snapped, his weapon aimed at Aaron and Felicia.

But Aaron's reflexes were quick. He had his own gun drawn in a flash. "Get out of our way, McMann. As you can see, your girlfriend doesn't have much time left. You'll want to say a quick goodbye."

Cade's furious blue gaze shifted past them to where she sat, strapped to the explosive device. Denial danced across his features before his mouth hardened with the determination she knew forged his soul.

"I slipped away from the deputies. You have less than five minutes before they figure out I came looking for a back entrance." His finger was steady on the trigger. "Disarm the bomb, and I'll let you go without a fight."

Instead of responding, Felicia finished tugging on the helmet, jammed the keys into the ignition and revved the engine. The huge warehouse's metal walls shook. With a nod to Aaron, she gunned the sports bike. The large machine lunged toward Cade.

Shots rang out.

Tori screamed.

The motorcycles sped through the door in single file, the angry sounds fading as shouting began outside the front of the building.

Cade lay unmoving on the floor, his eyes closed and his gun yards away on the oil-stained floor.

TWENTY

His chest felt like he'd been run over by an armored vehicle. He struggled to sit up.

"Cade! Can you hear me?"

Tori. He'd found her.

Bomb. There was a homemade explosive strapped to her.

"I'm okay," he managed to say, pushing to his knees. "They made me wear a Kevlar vest."

He heard her crying, and it spurred him to his feet. The shock of the close-range hit lingered, and there'd be major bruising, but he would live. They were both walking out of this warehouse.

He rushed to her side and bent to peer into her eyes. "We're going to figure this out."

Her hair was tangled, her clothes stained. There were the beginnings of fresh bruises on her neck, and an angry welt on her left cheek. Anger burned inside him. They would pay for hurting her.

"How did you find me?"

"Traffic cameras, for one. We also traced this warehouse to Maria's father, who's Felicia's uncle. It's remote. Made sense."

He gently wiped the moisture from her cheeks, bringing her focus to the bandages on his hands. "You're injured!"

"I had to destroy my coffee table in order to slice the ropes. The cuts are minor." He wouldn't have bothered with them, but Avery hadn't given him a choice.

"You have to leave, Cade."

"I'm not leaving you."

Her eyes bore a wealth of regret and urgency. "Take care of my mom. And Jason." A sob ripped from her throat. "Tell him I'm proud of him."

"Tell him yourself."

He checked the timer. Eight minutes. Fear coiled inside.

He dashed to the front entrance and hollered for help at the same time deputies entered the back door, weapons at the ready.

"We need someone to diffuse a bomb!"

They rushed over to inspect the device. Claxton and Avery joined them.

"The SWAT team can't make it in under fifteen minutes," Claxton said in a hushed voice, his normally stoic face pinched with worry.

Tori overheard. Though her eyes communicated fear, she didn't panic. "Leave me. That's your only choice."

"Out of the question." Cade went and crouched beside her chair. Studying the thick belt around her waist, he said, "We have to remove it."

Deputy Lewis, who'd accompanied them to the warehouse, moved closer to Tori, trying to get a better understanding of how the pipe was attached to the belt. He grimly nodded. "It'll be risky without knowing how well this thing was designed, but I agree."

"Our SWAT team members wouldn't approve, but

we're out of options." Claxton and Avery looked at each other. "Let's do it."

While the deputy went to fetch his tools, Cade gently cupped Tori's face. "Hang on, sweetheart. This will all be over in a few minutes."

A single tear snaked down her cheek. "Why do you have to be so stubborn?"

"I promised to protect you. This is me fulfilling that promise."

She glanced down at the device, a shudder racking her. "If this doesn't work—"

"It will."

He had to believe it. He wasn't naive. There was a chance jostling the homemade explosive would set off a reaction. Or cutting off the belt would release a hidden trigger. Without Felicia and Aaron here to give them answers, there was no way of knowing. But walking out of here, choosing his own safety while sacrificing hers, went against everything he stood for.

Pushing thoughts of his own family aside, he focused on Tori. His love for her gave him hope. It gave him courage.

Deputy Lewis returned with heavy-duty cutters. He advised everyone to vacate the building and move the cars. Claxton, Avery and another deputy did as he suggested. Cade didn't move.

"I don't have time to argue with you," Lewis informed him, his gaze serious and steady. "If you have any doubts about your decision, leave now."

"No doubts."

He shrugged. His calm and focus both impressed and reassured Cade. Both qualities were necessary to get the job done. After slicing through the thin ropes around Tori's torso, he turned his attention to the belt.

Cade checked the timer. Three minutes.

Sweat beaded on his forehead. The aches and pains plaguing his body faded as adrenalin flooded his system. He battered heaven with a litany of prayers. Selfish, desperate pleas. He knew God understood his heart.

"All right, I want you to slowly lift your arms," Lewis told Tori.

She did as he asked; her gaze locked with Cade's.

Lewis carefully sliced through the thick nylon material on one side of her waist. The tension of the belt slackened. Without thinking, Cade moved to balance the pipe. The deputy shot him an indecipherable glance.

"I'll remove it," Cade said. "Then you get her out of here."

Lewis didn't look pleased, but since Cade already had it in his hands, he nodded.

Tori protested.

"Two minutes," Cade pushed out. He gripped both ends of the pipe and, careful not to jostle it, eased the belt free. "Go!"

Lewis grabbed Tori's arm and hustled her to the door.

Keeping the pipe steady, Cade hurried to the far corner of the building and, crouching, set it on the floor. The ticking echoed in his head, his chances of getting clear of the building dwindling.

Releasing both ends, he raced for the nearest exit, praying he'd make it out in time.

An explosion shook the ground just as Tori and Deputy Lewis skidded behind a patrol vehicle. The initial blast was followed by a fireball. Debris pelted the ground.

Lewis shielded her head and back. When Tori tried to get a better look at the building, he grasped her wrist. "Stay down."

"But Cade—"

"We have to wait."

Her heart felt like it was going to beat out of her chest. Where *was* he?

Emotion clawed into her throat, making it hard to breathe.

He had to be okay. There were so many things she needed to say to him.

Seconds ticked by, the echoes of that terrible timer still in her head.

When the wait became too great, she tugged free of Lewis and scrambled to the front of the vehicle, ignoring his protest.

The warehouse was intact, but there was intense damage. Windows blown out. A portion of the metal roof ripped off. Smoke leaked out of the openings.

No sign of Cade.

On trembling legs, she advanced toward the building.

"You can't go in there, Miss James," Claxton called after her.

"Watch me," she muttered, not caring if he heard or not. They'd have to handcuff her, lock her in the back seat of a patrol car—

Movement in the trees grouped beside the warehouse's left exterior registered.

"Cade!"

A boost of energy lent her strength, and she ran to meet him, dodging smoldering shards of wood and metal.

He was limping. Bits of grass and leaves clung to his clothes and dirt smudged his face. But he was alive.

"Tori." Picking his way through the underbrush, he held his arms out.

She rushed into his embrace, burying her head in his chest and holding on for dear life. "I thought I'd lost you."

Hugging her close, he tenderly stroked her hair. "I'm not going to be easy to get rid of," he said huskily. "Not this time."

"The EMTs are two minutes out," Claxton called to them. "They'll want to transport you both to the hospital for complete evaluations."

Cade eased out of the embrace. "Any idea where Aaron and Felicia are headed?"

"Our guys are in pursuit and have contacted the Surf City PD. They're setting up roadblocks."

Deputy Lewis butted in. "I just received word they've split up. The female suspect has been spotted near the old gas station at Hickory Corner."

While Claxton was distracted, Cade touched Tori's shoulder. "That's less than ten miles from here. I'm going out there. I'll meet you at the hospital later."

Tori didn't bother trying to talk him out of it. This was personal for both of them. "You seriously think I'm going to let you go alone?"

"You were drugged, Tori."

"You were shot and very narrowly escaped an explosion, but we're still upright and functioning. The doctors can wait." Jerking a thumb over her shoulder, she said, "Your ride belongs to my brother, and you're not taking it without me."

"No time to argue. Let's go before anyone notices."

They were on the road and racing toward the highway when Cade's phone vibrated. He removed it from his pocket and handed it over.

"Claxton?" he said, his attention on his task.

She grimaced and nodded. "He won't be pleased."

Tori reluctantly answered and got a succinct warning… they weren't to approach the suspects for any reason.

"How do you know we aren't driving ourselves to the hospital?"

"I wasn't born yesterday," he groused, before ending the call.

Tori's gaze returned to Cade's profile. He'd survived despite the enemy's persistent attacks. God's hand of protection hadn't ever left them. It gave her courage now.

"Hold on." Cade executed a hairpin turn onto the highway heading toward Wilmington.

Minutes ticked by as the pine stands on either side of the highway became a greenish blur. Then he was turning again, this time onto a narrow road that, from the looks of things, didn't see much traffic. They hadn't traveled far when an oncoming pickup truck slammed on its brakes and waved them down.

Cade cracked his window open.

The driver, a thirtyish male with a heavy beard obscuring his features, gestured to the road behind him. "I'd turn around if I were you. A crazy woman tried to shoot me. All I did was offer her a ride."

"Can you give me a description?" Cade said.

His response painted a picture of a woman whose window of escape was narrowing. Felicia's motorcycle must've run out of gas or had engine problems.

"Thanks for the tip. The authorities are en route."

"She has to be getting desperate," Tori said when they'd left the truck behind. She scoured the woods for anything out of the ordinary. "Separated from her partner. No transportation. Police closing in."

His fingers tightened on the wheel. "Which makes her even more dangerous. The gas station is up ahead, on the right."

"There!" Tori slapped her palm flat against the window. "I saw something."

Cade jerked the car to the road's edge. "I guess it's too much to ask for you to stay here?"

"You guess right."

Emotion flared in his eyes and was quickly subdued. He killed the engine and handed her the keys. Together, they raced through the woods. A police helicopter buzzed overhead, flying low over the treetops.

They burst through the trees into a clearing at the same time the helicopter touched down not far from a dilapidated farmhouse. Felicia stood in the middle, her weapon trained on Cade and Tori.

"It's over, Felicia," Cade called, edging slightly in front of Tori.

Her dark eyes spewed hatred. "It'll never be over. Not for me."

"Have you ever asked yourself what William would think about all this?"

Her outstretched arm lowered a fraction.

"I didn't know him like you did, obviously." Cade edged another step to the right, almost completely blocking Felicia's view of Tori. "But I'm positive this woman you've become doesn't resemble the one he fell in love with."

Felicia licked her lips and blinked fast. Her stance faltered.

Members of the SWAT team exited the helicopter, weapons drawn, and fanned out into a semicircle behind her. Someone ordered her to lower hers. She didn't heed the command.

The blades slowed, and the air calmed. Tori's gaze bounced between the officers and Felicia. She was out of options.

"You thought that, by coming after us, you could somehow avenge his death," Cade said. "You should've been finding ways to honor the man and the Marine. His name's going to be in the news again, but not for noble reasons."

"No." Her brows descended, and she shook her head.

"You've brought dishonor to William's memory."

Felicia's face crumpled as a wail ripped from her lips. Her shoulders slumped.

The SWAT team took advantage of her distraction. There was a flurry of movement, and then she was disarmed and flat on the ground.

A team member approached and informed them that Aaron Waters was in custody, as well.

Cade folded Tori into his arms, his hand cradling her head to his chest. "It's over, sweetheart. It's finally over."

Back on the road, Deputy Claxton was waiting for them. His face a brewing storm, he looked them over. Was there a glimpse of relief in his implacable face?

"You two are going to get into my cruiser, and I'm going to personally deliver you to the hospital."

Cade's arm hadn't left her shoulders. "We appreciate the escort, sir."

"It's too late for the meek-mannered routine, Staff Sergeant."

"Yes, sir."

"But if you ever decide to switch careers, you should consider law enforcement. You'd be an asset to the sheriff's office."

Tori leaned into his side. "He's a Marine for life."

Cade gazed down at her, surprise giving way to hope. Tori had so many things to tell him, but it wasn't a conversation to have in the back of a police cruiser.

* * *

At the hospital, they were whisked to separate examination rooms. Jason burst into her room moments after the doctor cleared her.

"Tori, are you okay?" His eyes were wild. "I got a call from Brett an hour ago. When I went to the police station, they wouldn't tell me where you were or what was happening. Cade finally answered my texts and told me you'd been brought here."

Tori patted the edge of the mattress. "I'm sorry about that. Well, I'm not sorry they kept you away from the warehouse. There was a bomb—"

"A bomb?" He repeated, horrified.

"There wasn't time to disarm it, so Cade and Deputy Lewis cut the belt they'd used to strap it around me. They were the epitome of grace under fire—"

Her words were cut off when he wrapped his arms around her. Surprised, Tori didn't at first react. Jason used to be affectionate with her when he was younger. Before he became a teenager and it was no longer cool to like his sister.

"I'm glad you're safe, sis." His words were muffled.

She returned the embrace.

"Have they caught them yet?"

"They're both in custody." They wouldn't have to live in fear and uncertainty anymore. "I'm glad you're here, Jason. There are a few things I'd like to say."

He stood, his gaze growing wary. "Now? Shouldn't you be resting or something?"

"I should've done this long before now. I'm sorry I hurt you. That wasn't my intention. I left Sneads Ferry because of my broken engagement, and then I got comfortable in my new life. I thought visiting you a couple of times a year was enough. That cards and emails and text messages were enough." He seemed preoccupied with the view outside the window. Was he tuning her out? "I was your age when I started over in Tennessee. I was focused on myself and my future, not my eight-year-old brother. Can you try to put yourself in my shoes?"

He was quiet for a long beat. "I guess I can understand that." He slid his attention to her. "I wouldn't let a younger sibling stop me from pursuing my dreams."

"The older I got, the more I missed you and Mom. I decided to come home partly because it would allow us to rebuild our relationship."

"You asked me to put myself in your shoes. Are you willing to do the same for me?" He pushed off the wall and spread his hands. "I'm not happy at the factory. I want more."

She smoothed the thin sheet covering her. "I was wrong to try to dissuade you, Jason. I was being selfish, and I'm sorry."

His pale brows shot up. "You're giving me your blessing?"

"I'm proud of your willingness to serve. I think you'll make a fine Marine. I love you, Jason. I know you don't want to hear this mushy stuff, but I have to say what's on my heart."

"Love you, too." He scrubbed the tile with his tennis shoe. "And I'm glad you're home. Maybe we can go see a movie sometime."

It was the olive branch she'd been hoping for.

"I'd like that."

Her mother arrived, tearful and overwrought, and the explanations started all over again. Barbara felt terrible about letting Felicia into their lives. Tori reassured her that she wasn't to blame. No one had seen through her solicitous act to the deranged woman beneath.

* * *

Cade came to her room at last and, after accepting hugs from her mother and brother, asked Tori to walk with him. He looked adorably rumpled, fatigue an invisible mantle that couldn't detract from his steadfast strength. He absently rubbed his chest and winced. She'd seen the nasty bruises and thanked the Lord he'd done as the deputies asked and put on a bulletproof vest.

They found their way to a deserted courtyard.

"Alone at last." She sighed. "I feel like I've been waiting years to say this." Tori lifted her gaze. His eyes were a beautiful, deep navy against his sun-kissed skin. She'd come so close to losing him, forever.

"I want you to know I'm not going anywhere," she told him, her voice husky with emotion. "Not like last time."

Lips parting, Cade's gaze probed hers. "What are you saying?"

She smiled tremulously up at him. "It's simple, really. I love you, Cade. I want to be with you, whether it's in Sneads Ferry or Japan or Antarctica. Doesn't matter, as long as we're together, building the life we dreamed about all those years ago."

His throat worked. "Are you one hundred percent certain? Because once we make it official, I'm never letting you go, Victoria James."

Joy bloomed in her heart. "I'm ready for the challenges *and* the adventures. My parents' troubles and Brett's heartache doesn't have to be our experience. I was focused on the negative to the point I forgot about the blessings of military life—the unbelievably strong support system, the knowledge that you're part of something bigger than yourself. Military members and their families are connected by shared experiences, and that's a unique bond that can't be duplicated."

His crooked smile thrilled her to her toes. "You forgot about the perks like cheap, on-base movies."

"Tax-free shopping."

"Friends all over the globe."

"Friends that become family." She wrapped her arms around his neck. "Most importantly, my very own hero."

He turned serious. "I love you, Tori."

Cade dipped his head. His kiss was fierce yet tender and charged with emotion that brought fresh tears to her eyes. She'd never cease being grateful for God's deliverance. And for a second chance with Cade.

EPILOGUE

Six months later

For the first time since their wedding four months ago, Cade didn't rush home, eager to see Tori and hear about her day. He'd known this day would come. He'd hoped it would be further into the future.

"Cade?" she called. "I'm in the kitchen."

The rich, buttery aroma of baked goods intensified as he got closer. Turning the corner, he smiled at the sight of her painstakingly icing a cookie shaped like a candy cane. From the looks of things, she'd been baking the entire day.

Straightening, she greeted him with a smile that never failed to melt him. "Hey. How was work?"

He walked around the center island and greeted her with a kiss. "You're sweeter than usual," he teased, wiping a smudge of yellow icing from the corner of her mouth. "How many of these have you had?"

Their kitchen looked like the Christmas command center. Piping bags full of brightly colored icing, bottles of sprinkles and candies shaped like miniature trees and candy canes crowded the space. Painted tins lined with tissue waited to be filled with Tori's homemade treats.

"Three." Her green eyes danced with mischief.

He wagged his finger. "I don't believe you."

"Four. Definitely four."

He snagged a star-shaped sugar cookie, bit into it and groaned. "No way you stopped at four, dear wife."

"To be honest, I stopped counting after the fifth one." After laying aside the piping bag, she washed her hands at the window sink and poured him a tall glass of milk. "Lenore was supposed to come and help, but the baby's sick so she had to cancel."

At the mention of Lenore, a fellow staff sergeant's wife and Tori's new friend, Cade's misgivings returned full force. Since getting involved with the Family Readiness Group, Tori had met many military wives. She'd taken to life as a military spouse far quicker than he'd anticipated. He was proud of her. That's why telling her the news wasn't going to be easy.

Eating more cookies seemed like a good way to stall.

Tori tilted her head to one side, her shiny hair brushing the underside of her chin. "Is something bothering you?"

"Why do you ask?"

"You avoided my question about work."

He downed half the glass and set it aside. "Maybe I don't have any interesting stories to share today."

Her expression said she didn't buy it. Folding her arms over her gingerbread-emblazoned apron, she said, "You can tell me anything." A furrow dug between her pale brows. "It's not Julian, is it? The surgery was a success, right?"

He sighed, thinking of the tragic helicopter accident that had left his friend in bad shape. Cade was afraid the emotional challenges would far exceed the physical. "He's going to recover."

"But his future in Special Forces is uncertain."

"His future as a Marine," he amended. Going out on clandestine missions was out of the question. "It's a game of wait and see."

"I put him on the church's prayer list."

Crossing to her, Cade looped his arms around her waist. "That was nice. Thank you."

She rested her hands on his biceps and waited.

"They need me in Camp Pendleton," he blurted, and then held his breath.

Her eyes widened. "California?"

"I'm to report there in two months." He glanced around at the house she'd put her own stamp on. "I'm sorry, Tori. I wasn't expecting it this soon. You'll have to leave our church and the new friends you've made. Angela and your mom."

Surveying the kitchen, she slowly smiled. "You're right, I will miss this house and everything else. But I won't have to worry about my mom, now that your mom has retired and is pitching in to help. Dee told me that your cousin will start work at the shop after graduation in May. Besides, I've never been to the West Coast. Think of all the places we'll get to visit."

The vise in Cade's chest eased its grip. "You're not upset?"

"Lenore gave me an important piece of advice—in the military, you've got to bloom where you're planted. God's uprooting us for a season. One day, we'll wind up back here."

"You're right about that."

Not only would they likely be stationed here again, but they'd have to return in coming months to testify at Heath's, Aaron's and Felicia's trials. Tori's strength and resiliency were impressive.

"We'll be closer to Jason," she said excitedly. After

completing basic training and the school of infantry, he'd been assigned to Twentynine Palms, California. Not a favorite place for most guys, but Jason seemed to be content. He kept in touch with emails and frequent video chats.

"And who knows." She trailed her fingers up and over his shoulders, the delicate touch sending a cascade of goose bumps across his skin. "There might be surfer babies in our future."

The thought of having a child with Tori filled him with awe and wonder. "I like the sound of that," he murmured, pulling her closer. "I'm one blessed man to have you in my life."

She beamed with happiness. "You're my home, Cade. Not this house or this town. *You.*"

His heart so full that he couldn't speak, Cade offered up a prayer of thanksgiving and kissed his wife. Sometimes dreams faded. And sometimes dreams changed and became bigger, better, brighter. He was living his dream at last.

* * * * *

Dear Reader,

What a roller-coaster ride this book journey has been! In the spring of this year, after having written multiple books for Love Inspired Historical, I learned the sad news of the line's closing. After much prayer, I turned my sights on the romantic suspense line and was grateful my editor agreed to let me submit an idea. The appeal of the military hero was strong. My husband and I lived the military life for nearly eight years. The challenges were many and varied, but so were the blessings. Writing about Camp Lejeune and the surrounding areas, and about the brave men and women who serve, brought back many wonderful memories. I've had such fun writing this story, and I hope to return to this setting in future books.

I love to hear from readers. You can find me on Facebook and Twitter. My website, www.karenkirst.com, has information about my historical romances, including my Smoky Mountain Matches series. I will update it with information about my new romantic suspense adventures. You can also email me at karenkirst@live.com.

Thank you for choosing my book.

Blessings,
Karen Kirst

Get 4 FREE REWARDS!

We'll send you 2 FREE Books plus 2 FREE Mystery Gifts.

Love Inspired® Suspense books feature Christian characters facing challenges to their faith... and lives.

FREE Value Over $20

"I have your new identities." US marshal Jonathan Mast
sat across the table from Julia in the hotel where she and
her children had been holed up for the last five days.

The Luchadors wanted to kill William so he wouldn't
testify against their leader. As much as Julia didn't trust
law enforcement, she had to rely on the US Marshals and
their witness protection program to keep her family safe.
No wonder her nerves were stretched thin.

"We're ready to transport you and the children,"
Jonathan Mast continued. "We'll fly into Kansas City
tonight, then drive to Topeka and north to Yoder."

"What's in Kansas?"

Jonathan pulled out his phone and accessed a
photograph. He handed the cell to Julia. "Abraham King
will watch over you in Kansas."

Julia studied the picture. The man looked to be in his midthirties with a square face and deep-set eyes beneath dark brows. His nose appeared a bit off center, as if it had been broken. Lips pulled tight and no hint of a smile on his angular face.

"Mr. King doesn't look happy."

Jonathan shrugged. "Law enforcement photos are never flattering."

Her stomach tightened. "He's a cop?"

"Past tense. He left the force three years ago."

Once a cop, always a cop. Her ex had been a police officer. He'd protected others but failed to show that same sense of concern when it came to his own family. The marshal seemed oblivious to her unease.

"Abe is an old friend," Jonathan continued. "A widower from my police-force days who owns a farm and has a spare house on his property. He lives in a rural Amish community."

"Amish?"

"That's right."

"Bonnets and buggies?" she asked.

He smiled weakly. "You'll be off the grid, Mrs. Bradford. No one will look for you there."

Don't miss
Amish Safe House *by Debby Giusti,*
available February 2019 wherever
Love Inspired® Suspense books and ebooks are sold.

www.LoveInspired.com

Looking for inspiration in tales
of hope, faith and heartfelt romance?

Check out **Love Inspired**® and
Love Inspired® **Suspense** books!

New books available every month!

CONNECT WITH US AT:

Facebook.com/groups/HarlequinConnection

 Facebook.com/HarlequinBooks

 Twitter.com/HarlequinBooks

 Instagram.com/HarlequinBooks

 Pinterest.com/HarlequinBooks

ReaderService.com

Love Inspired®

LIGENRE2018R2

Inspirational Romance to Warm Your Heart and Soul

Join our social communities to connect
with other readers who share your love!

Sign up for the Love Inspired newsletter
at **www.LoveInspired.com** to be the
first to find out about upcoming titles,
special promotions and exclusive content.

CONNECT WITH US AT:

Facebook.com/groups/HarlequinConnection

 Facebook.com/LoveInspiredBooks

 Twitter.com/LoveInspiredBks

LISOCIAL2018